Owl in Love

Other Graphia Titles

COMFORT
by Carolee Dean

3 NBS OF JULIAN DREW
by James M. Deem

48 SHADES OF BROWN
by Nick Earls

DUNK
by David Lubar

ZAZOO
by Richard Mosher

———————————

Check out www.graphiabooks.com

Owl in Love

PATRICE KINDL

AN IMPRINT OF HOUGHTON MIFFLIN COMPANY
Boston

www.houghtonmifflin.com
Graphia and the Graphia logo are trademarks of Houghton Mifflin Company.

Library of Congress Cataloging-in-Publication Data
Kindl, Patrice.
  Owl in love / Patrice Kindl.
    p. cm
  Summary: A fourteen-year-old girl, who can transform into an
owl, has a crush on her science teacher which leads her into inter-
esting new relationships with both humans and owls.
  (HC) ISBN 0-395-66162-5
  (PB) ISBN 0-618-43910-2
  {1. Supernatural—Fiction.   2. Owls—Fiction.   3. Teacher-
student relationships—Fiction.}   I. Title.
PZ7.K56650w   1993   92-26952
{Fic}—dc20   CIP
                    AC
Printed in the United States of America
HAD 10 9 8 7 6 5 4 3 2 1

To Kandy, without whom this book
would have been written in half the time,
and to Paul and Alex,
just because I love them.

One

I AM IN LOVE with Mr. Lindstrom, my science teacher. I found out where he lives and every night I perch on a tree branch outside his bedroom window and watch him sleep. He sleeps in his underwear: Fruit of the Loom, size 34.

I watch him while I should be hunting. When I don't hunt, I don't eat. I grow thin for love of Mr. Lindstrom. My parents are getting worried. I go to bed at dawn, after watching Mr. Lindstrom as he sleeps all night. Then my parents tiptoe in and watch anxiously as I sleep. It's only fair, I suppose.

I am not stupid, you know. I read teen magazines like *Seventeen* and *Sassy,* just like other girls. I know what *Psychology Today* has to say about young girls (I turned fourteen last June) who fall in love with their science teachers. Mr. Lindstrom is not a substitute for my father. He is nothing like my father. My father is pale as a potato sprouting in a root cellar; Mr. Lindstrom is red and brown and furry like the flanks of a deer mouse.

Yes, and the magazines hint that a teacher is a safe object of desire for a girl not yet ready to date a boy her own age. Mr. Lindstrom is available, they would say, but not too available. He is near enough that I can count every pore on his nose, thrill to the sweat stains under his jacket on a hot September day, tremble at his small kindnesses to me. Ah, the low rumble of his voice when he is amused! Like the sweet threat of thunder on a sultry summer's day. O Mr. Lindstrom!

But I digress.

They would maintain, these ladies and gentlemen who are so wise about young girls, that because Mr. Lindstrom is forty years old, has a receding hairline and a mortgage on a split-level in Hillcrest Estates, he is unobtainable, out of the reach of a girl not yet full grown, and therefore safe.

Is It Really Love? they would demand, with an unbelieving sniff. I think it must be, but how can I tell? I am so inexperienced in these matters. All I know is that it is no small thing. I am consumed; I am eaten up with desire for him. If this is what is called "just" a crush, I shudder to imagine the staggering weight of the real thing.

It is true that I would very much like Mr. Lindstrom to kiss me. If this suggests that my longings are for the flesh rather than the spirit, I have no defense. I can sit and dream up stories by the hour, stories that detail every precious moment leading up to that fated kiss. What happens next is a little vague, I confess. A casual affair is simply out of the question; it is marriage or nothing for me. Yet how can that be? It would not be legal in this state, not for another year and a half, even with parental consent. It is a long time to wait.

I can tell you this: other teenage girls are said to suffer from "crushes" for a week, a month, a year. Then one day they look at their beloved and they begin to giggle. The madness has passed. They even blush to remember their passion. This will not happen to me. It is not in my nature. If Mr. Lindstrom never returns my love, the next sixty or seventy years of my life will be a heavy burden indeed. Yes, of course I know that in seventy years Mr. Lindstrom would be a hundred and ten, but with my love to nourish him, why should he not live beyond the normal span of years?

Mr. Lindstrom is free to marry, I know. A girl who lives in Hillcrest Estates (it was she who told me where he lives) said that six months ago his wife took the Pontiac Gran Prix and screeched out of the driveway so fast she left a two-foot stack of Johnny Mathis records, a tennis racket, and tire tracks on the blacktop. She has never come back.

Poor Mr. Lindstrom! It is obvious that he lives alone and does not like it. He is getting a crumpled, dingy look, and his eyes are hurt and surprised.

It is not usual for science teachers to marry students twenty-six years younger than themselves, but I am not the usual fourteen-year-old either. I don't say this to boast; it is simply true.

I am Owl. It is my name as well as my nature. There are birds of prey in my family going back hundreds of years, one every two or three generations. Others of my family shift to dog- or cat-kind, a few to hoofed or finned beasts.

Let me be clear. I would not wish you to misunderstand: by night I seek my living in owl shape, among the fields and woods surrounding my home. By day I am an ordinary girl (more or less) attending the local high school. I am no vampire in a fairy tale, to be ruled by the sun or moon; I can shift to either shape at any time of night or day.

My mother and father are not shapeshifters. They are simple witches, dabbling in such little arts as they can command: weather, prophecy, herbal healing. They are the best and kindest of parents to me. I grieve to think how they suffer now because of my sufferings.

Life is a strange and sometimes terrible thing.

If Mr. Lindstrom had not as a boy loved dinosaurs and chemistry sets, he would never have become a science teacher, never have come here to teach me biology and trouble my nights. Sometimes, seeing my dear parents growing nearly transparent with worry, watching them as they drift aimlessly through the halls of our ancestral home, up and down the staircases, wringing their white hands, I wish that young Mr. Lindstrom had chosen to collect stamps instead of butterflies.

My fellow students at Wildewood Senior High have always thought me strange, odd. They are right. I am very different from them. My blood, for instance, is black, while theirs is red. It is a pretty color, human blood, when it is fresh. I have always had to be very careful not to injure myself when others might be watching. I am nimble and have a good head for heights (naturally), so I have had little trouble.

Mr. Lindstrom wants us to prick our fingers tomorrow in science class and squeeze one drop of blood out onto a glass slide, so that we can test it for blood groupings. If only he had asked for anything else of mine but that! Even my blood I would give him, to the last pint, if it would make him happy. But will it? I doubt it. I don't know what to do. I may ask another pupil to donate some of her or his blood to my slide. It is difficult though. Because I am different I do not make friends easily.

O positive. AB negative. What combination of letters could describe my blood grouping? They would be letters in no human alphabet, I think.

How odd to think that Mr. Lindstrom has bright scarlet blood like the others running in his veins, coloring his cheeks. Still, where there is no light there is no color, so within the dark fortress of his body his blood is as black as mine. In the night we are kin, Mr. Lindstrom and I.

Sometimes I would like not to be what I am.

As a child I was teased by the other children and pestered by the grownups for never bringing a lunch of my own to school or eating the hot lunch provided. My coloring in health is naturally gray rather than rosy, and this convinced them all that I was at death's door, entirely owing to my refusal to eat the "nice ravioli" or pizza or whatever disgusting messes the school kitchen produced.

My diet is largely composed of small rodents and insects. I can hardly lunch on grasshoppers before the eyes of several hundred ninth-graders, so I prefer not to eat lunch at all. Besides, it is unnatural for an owl to be awake at noon (though not so unusual as some people imagine), and a heavy meal makes it all the harder to concentrate upon my studies.

Even more to the point, if I were to eat human food I would lose the ability to fly, even the ability to transform to owl shape. Just a few bites would not do much harm, but the more I eat, the more obstinately human I become.

One day a few weeks ago, shortly after I realized that I was hopelessly in love with Mr. Lindstrom, a girl jeered at my solitary, lunchless state in the cafeteria. I had been feeling rather low-spirited over my chances with Mr.

Lindstrom, and this unkindness was like the straw in the proverb which broke the camel's back.

The barren, desert distances that separated Mr. Lindstrom and me seemed to stretch to truly Sahara-like proportions. Not only are we of different generations, but we do not even belong to the same species. No, nor do we belong to the same genus, family, order, or class. We share membership only in the animal kingdom and in the phylum Chordata, which means that we both possess a backbone. The most that can be said for our common ground is that we are more like one another than we are like amoebas, sponges, snails, or earthworms. What odds, I wonder, would the ladies of *Seventeen* and *Sassy* give on a romance like that?

And then that unpleasant female reminded me of yet another trouble. In the language of love, an invitation to dine in the company of the beloved is an unspoken offer of greater intimacy. It is as true of owls as of human beings. In owl courtship the male tenderly feeds his lady a mouse with the head torn off or some other similarly tempting tidbit. This traditional engagement gift is more than can reasonably be expected of Mr. Lindstrom, but food is clearly a key ingredient to romance. How could I manage a closer relationship without at some time eating in his presence?

A little disguise might help, I thought. Next day I took

7

a tasty little mouse and laid it between two slices of white bread (my parents prefer a more conventional diet than I, so there is plenty of human food in the house). I wrapped this bundle, as I have observed is the custom, in a sheet of plastic. I placed it in a small brown paper bag and enclosed a paper napkin. With the opening sealed by a fold, and my name, "OWL," printed neatly across it, it looked quite typical, if a little skimpy in size and weight.

My fellow scholars noticed long before lunch. As soon as I arrived at school, I took it out of my tote bag and put it, rather self-consciously, in my locker.

"Hey!" yelled Steve Moran, whose locker is about five feet away from mine. "Owl's got a lunch today!"

A small crowd collected at once. I shut the door to my locker immediately, but it was too late. Most of these people and I had gone to grade school and middle school together. They knew that I never, ever, under any circumstances, brought a lunch.

"What ya bring fer lunch, Owl? Birdseed?" demanded one witty soul. My classmates had long ago spotted the similarity between my name and my physical appearance. My face is wide and heart-shaped, with very large yellow eyes in which the irises are so big that the whites can barely be seen. I have the kind of hairline which comes to a sharp point in the center of the forehead, known as a widow's peak, and my hair falls in soft, feathery, brown wisps around my neck and shoulders. In short, I look like an owl in human form—not so strikingly that anyone has ever guessed my dual nature, but enough to cause comment.

You will notice how ignorant they are about the feeding habits of owls. Birdseed! As if I were a parakeet!

When they tired of teasing me, I moved on to my homeroom, hoping to have heard the last of it. Unfortunately, the entire student body seemed starved for entertainment. They fixed on my small departure from normal routine, and I had to put up with a good deal of chitchat and foolishness on the subject.

"BuckbuckbuckBUCK!" clucked several boys in my first period, now apparently under the impression that I was a hen. "Time to feed the chickens, Paw!" "Ay-yup! Git the lunch bag, Maw!" The entry of Mrs. Gaines restored order, but an undercurrent of giggling ran through that and every class up until lunchtime.

At lunch the tension was high. I nearly left the little brown bag, now grown hateful to me, in my locker. If necessary, I could explain that it had contained art materials or equipment for a science project. The problem of what to do about dining with Mr. Lindstrom still haunted me, however, so I took it out and brought it with me to the cafeteria. Besides all other considerations, it seemed a shame to waste such a good mouse.

It was a sensation. My audience was not only the ninth grade but any from the upper grades who could manage to peep around the cafeteria doors during my lunch hour, not to mention teachers, staff, and administrators, who had no proper business in the area at the time except to gawk at a girl eating her lunch. I withdrew my sandwich and pried it out of the confining plastic with fingers grown clumsy from nerves. I was very careful to pinch the edges of the bread together so that no hint of the filling (especially the tail or whiskers) could be seen.

Under the gaze of half a thousand eyes I ate the sandwich, brushed the crumbs from my lap, dabbed at my mouth with the paper napkin, and disposed of my trash in the can provided. Then I got out my books as I normally do and began to study for a Spanish test scheduled for that afternoon.

In some ways the experiment was a success; in some ways it was a failure.

It was a success in the sense that most of my onlookers seemed to think I had scored some kind of a point. Since that day no one, either student or teacher or staff, has annoyed me on the subject of eating lunch.

On the other hand it was a failure for two reasons. One, it has occurred to me that it is entirely unreasonable to expect a romantic little French bistro or, indeed, any sort of dining establishment, to offer curried mouse or cricket à la king or anything else I would find fit to eat. A picnic lunch, prepared by myself, would be the best I could manage. Perhaps my mother would help me with the menu for Mr. Lindstrom's share of the meal.

The second cause for my sense of failure lay in the physical sensations I experienced after the lunch period. I have been raised exclusively on the diet appropriate for an owl. I had hoped that this slight deviation from the norm would not cause me any difficulties, but it did.

The bread, which after all is a strange food, made of a paste of grasses and greases swollen with the gassy emissions of yeast plants, sat very heavily upon my stomach. It seemed to swell until I felt as though I had swallowed a whole loaf instead of two thin slices.

Flying was out of the question that night. I might as well have leapt from the rooftop with a hundred-pound boulder strapped to my chest. It was several days before I felt anything like normal in my lower regions. Never more, I vowed. Not unless my conquest of Mr. Lindstrom's heart absolutely depended upon it would human fare pass my lips.

• • •

Always and forever, he fell, a dark meteor streaking down the sky. Falling, he screamed, and fell again. So it ever was, so it ever shall be: the falling, the dark, the scream.

In the grip of this threefold terror, his mind struggled briefly. Had there not been a time, long ago and in another place, when it was different? When he did not fall but sailed on the shadowy arm of night, shaping the wind with mind and muscle? Wasn't there, behind the fear, some great joy?

Perhaps it was true, but there was no use remembering that now. That was the time, so long ago, before he had understood his own evil nature, before he knew himself a dark angel cast out of the sky, out of joy. That was before his mind had broken under the weight of self-knowledge.

Yet just for a moment, his thoughts stirred, beat the air. He hung suspended in the sky, his eternal descent arrested. How silent it was! Below, far, far below, a sound. A slight . . . rustle. Yes!

He screamed. And fell into darkness.

"He's done it again. See, it's all over the place."

The drug-soaked dreams tried to reclaim him, even as he was shaken, not roughly, not gently.

"Wake up."

His eye opened a slit. There was blood on the pillowcase. A warm liquid filled his mouth, tasting of salt and iron. His mouth was full of blood. Yes. He smiled. That was what he had dreamed of: blood in his mouth.

TWO

My parents have given me permission to marry Mr. Lindstrom. It is very sweet of them, but I'm afraid they have little practical understanding of the laws of New York State or of the true nature of my problem.

"Of course you must marry anyone you like!" They hugged me, then each other, and laughed. Tenderly my father wiped the tears of relief from my mother's face. "Oh, Owl, we were so frightened!"

My passion for Mr. Lindstrom is the first secret I have ever intentionally kept from my parents. I confessed now because I could not bear to think that I was causing them such pain. Besides, that mournful creak on the stairs, the soft, padded drag of their feet as they crept through the halls, the weight of their anxious eyes upon me as I slept, all of these things were beginning to get on my nerves.

I felt a curious shyness in the telling that I had never before known with my parents. My neck and cheeks were strangely warm, and I found it difficult to meet their eyes. I cannot understand why this should be. My parents love each other devotedly, and of course one of their fondest hopes for me is that I should find a love as true as their own. Yet I mumble and duck my head as I speak of it before them.

Why should I be ashamed of a need that ought to be as simple, as commonplace, as hunger or thirst? Why have I grown so odd?

My mother became sentimental. "Owl is in love, Papa. In love! Our baby." As if remembering her own courtship, she slipped her arm through my father's and snuggled up to him.

"Of course, we will want to meet this young man," my father said, as sternly as any man can while his wife is nibbling on his ear.

"Oh! The wedding!" My mother cried out as if she had been stung. "We'll have it here, of course." She dropped my father's arm and backed up against the fireplace to get a better view of the room.

"Hmmm," she said thoughtfully. "Hmmm . . ." She shook her head, the excitement leaking from her like air from a punctured balloon. "Oh dear," she murmured faintly. "Oh dear! Not quite exactly . . . is it?"

She looked so woebegone that my father lost some of his proud-father-of-the-bride glow and began to look nervously around the familiar room. "Something wrong, Nesta? Looks very nice, I always think." He rubbed his long, thin hands together and cracked his knuckles hopefully.

It should have been funny. I bought a *Bride* magazine the other day at the supermarket, and I know the sort of home they mean when they say, "The bride was married from her home." Those homes *always* have running water and electricity, not to mention rugs and furniture and pictures on the wall. Not that we have no furniture at all. We have our beds; one for me and a big old four-poster for my parents. There is a table in the dining room and one in the kitchen, a nice big one, and we each have a chair. It is enough.

Then too, we keep most of the shutters closed so that the neighborhood children cannot look in, which makes it rather dark, even in the daytime. I prefer the darkness, and luckily, it suits my parents as well.

The big, high-ceilinged, empty rooms—there are eighteen or nineteen, I think—are a wonderful place for an owl. It was there that I learned to fly and there that I still fly on bitter cold winter nights, hunting the mice and occasional rats that creep in through the cracks.

I say it should have been funny, comparing our grand (but admittedly dark and empty) mansion with the homes of the magazine brides. Yet I was not amused. For the first time in my life, I found myself growing irritated with my mother and father. Their innocence, which usually I find so touching, annoyed rather than pleased me. It was very ungrateful of me, but I'm afraid my love for Mr. Lind-strom is making me unreasonable.

I found myself speaking quite sharply to my poor mother. "Oh, Mother! Don't be so stupid!" I snapped and turned abruptly away.

Mother and Father stared at me, confused, frightened. I could not meet their eyes but stood, stirring a little heap of dead leaves and mouse remains with the toe of my athletic shoe, half remorseful, half defiant.

"Darling, what is it?"

"My dear girl, you can tell us! How are we being stupid?"

In my misery I blurted out, "He doesn't want to marry me. He barely knows I exist! And even if he did, even if he loved me, we couldn't be married legally. I'm underage."

My parents were utterly baffled. As parents go they are more fond than wise. They could understand none of it. How anyone I loved could not love me in return, could not desire our marriage as passionately as I, was entirely beyond them. And as for the role of the state of New York in thwarting young love, they simply shook their heads in wonderment.

"The wickedness of it!" my mother whispered in awe. "To think how they demand all that tax money every year, hundreds and hundreds of dollars! Money scraped together with so much hardship . . ." Mother's lips trembled, and her fingers worried at the frayed hem of her apron, thinking, I knew, of the stacks of nickels and dimes, little mounds of one- and five- and ten-dollar bills. "And now we find out the sort of laws that our money goes to support! It's . . . it's villainous!"

"Actually," my father, who is a fair man, corrected her, "it isn't the state that wants that money every year. They know our income is too small to tax. It's the town that sends the policeman out to collect the property tax."

My family is not wealthy, though historically some generations have been very prosperous. My mother has a large vegetable and herb garden in the back yard, and she cans enough to fill most of my parents' nutritional needs for the year. Flour for bread and a few other staples are all they need at the supermarket. I am able to contribute fresh meat several times a week, usually mice, although they are delighted with the occasional rabbit I can snare. I feed myself quite adequately without assistance.

For the rest, they both visit the dump on a regular basis, gleaning all sorts of odds and ends that can be put to good use. The attics are filled with furniture, some of it valuable, which can be sold in an emergency. There are trunks of clothing up there as well, which are made over by my mother's nimble needle to fit us all. Much of the clothing is well over a hundred years old. This may explain why we look, as the clerk at the Shop 'n' Save says, "so sort of quaint."

The nickels and dimes and paper money come in through the kitchen door, the bills tightly rolled and damp with nervous sweat. They come because of the sign at the back door which reads:

HERBAL REMEDIES
—NATURE'S OWN CURE—
FRESH VEGETABLES IN SEASON.

Generally people send their children around, with an order like "A pound of tomatoes, please, and Mom says can she have some more of the usual. She says you'll know what she means."

The "usual" can be anything from rheumatism salve to a "Tonic for Tired Husbands." Young people, and some who are no longer young, come looking for love potions. Businesspeople want money spells, expectant mothers ask for knot charms against pain, brides want blue skies for their weddings, and the anxious (or bored) want to have their fortunes told.

The money spell works, if not very spectacularly. My father keeps one in our little metal cash box and, as he says, we never lack for anything we truly want or need. It does not seem to be very good at producing anything beyond the essentials, however.

The money spell in fact works better than some of the others. My parents are very, very honest. They would never sell a charm, no, not the merest good-luck piece, if they did not believe it gave value for money. On the other hand, they are both blessed with an optimistic and uncritical nature, so they are able to offer quite a large line of goods with a clear conscience. The laws of chance and probability do not worry them much.

"'There are more things in heaven and earth, Horatio, than are dreamt of in your philosophy,'" is my mother's answer to any criticisms, quoting the poet Shakespeare.

"'A foolish consistency is the hobgoblin of little minds,'" adds my father, in the words of the great American philosopher Emerson.

Thus lightly do they dismiss logic and even science, that discipline in which Mr. Lindstrom so distinguishes himself. Out of loyalty to him, I sometimes attempt to reason with them. The magazine writers inform me that similar values and interests are very important in a relationship. Unfortunately my own dual nature defies rational explanation, which makes it difficult for me to argue the scientific viewpoint very convincingly. There are other laws, it seems, which are both subtler and stranger than the laws of reason.

My father was looking thoughtful. His bony fingers plucked unhappily at the thin braid of gray hair that straggles down his neck. Finally he thrust the end of the braid into his mouth and began to chew on it, a sure sign of mental distress.

"Perhaps, sweetie," my father suggested hesitantly, "he is not the right one for you?"

Before I could reassure him, my father continued, his steel-wool eyebrows bunching fiercely over his nose, "A man so thickheaded, so boorish, as not to appreciate your fine qualities? What sort of a man is that, after all? The swine," he growled, warming to his theme. "He ought not to be allowed to teach sensitive young girls. Trifling with their hearts in this callous way! Why, the man ought to be dismissed from his job at the high school!"

"Daddy!" I cried, horrified. "How *dare* you say these things about the man I love with all my heart and soul! Remember who I am. I am Owl; it is in my nature to give my love once and only once in a lifetime. I shall love him until I die, or he does."

My father folded his arms across his chest and frowned down at me. "The last part could be arranged," he said darkly.

"Fritz!" shrieked my mother in protest.

I did not speak; I merely looked at him.

He groaned, and passed a hand over his face. "Baby,

I'm sorry. I know what you say is true. But when I think of that man, having the *gall* to treat you so! How could it not make a father's blood boil?"

My mother put an arm around my shoulder. "Hush, Fritz! You should be ashamed to speak of our future son-in-law so." She whispered in my ear, "He's just jealous, Owl. Fathers are always like that when they have to give up their baby girl. Now come into the kitchen and tell me all about him. I want to know every single detail."

So I told her every single detail. I told her about his hair, his eyes, his smile, the way he walks, the nick in his chin he gave himself shaving this morning. I reported on his jokes, his taste in sweaters, the long hairs in his nose, what he said today about the international situation, how his left shoe has a small hole starting right up near the big toe—everything.

My foolish embarrassment vanished. I found great relief in being able to speak of him openly. It was rather difficult to stop. Even after my parents had eaten and I had completed my homework, at an hour when I normally retire for a few hours of sleep before going hunting, I still sat talking. I who rarely speak more than a handful of words in the course of a day, I prattled, I chattered, I babbled like a brook.

After three hours I had sketched in the outlines of his portrait, but I still had much to say. By this time, however, I was as hoarse as a crow and, to a sensitive eye, it was obvious that even my indulgent mother was ready for a change of subject.

She had leaned back in her chair, her head against my father's shoulder. Her eyes were shut—to concentrate better, I suppose—but she seemed weary to me.

My father sat bolt upright and stared moodily off into the scullery. He was sulking simply because Mr. Lindstrom had formed the sole topic of conversation for the evening. Remembering his cruel speech earlier, I ignored his ill humor and continued my remarks.

At last my mother stirred and, yawning (you see I was right about her being tired), said, "Perhaps you had better go to bed, dear, so as to be fresh for the night's hunt. And be sure you do go hunting! Don't just watch Mr. Lindstrom all night!"

"Did I tell you that he hardly ever snores? Only when he gets on his stomach sometimes he makes this tiny little sound . . . I don't know how to describe it exactly, like dead leaves scuffling along the ground—"

"If you can hear him through two panes of glass, perched on a tree limb, what, ten feet away? he must have a snore like a freight train," my father interrupted rudely.

"Mother," I said coldly, "would you please tell Father that I, like all owls, have exceptionally fine hearing? I should think it would be something of which he would already be aware."

"Oh, dear," Mother said. "Do go to bed, Owl. You'll be worn to a frazzle tonight otherwise."

I left with dignity, kissing my mother with more than my usual affection and neglecting to kiss my father at all. My father made some sort of growling noise as I left the room. Very unlike him; he is usually such a quiet, loving man. My mother must be right. He is jealous of Mr. Lindstrom. How silly!

I took my mother's advice. Refreshed by four hours' sleep and feeling much happier since our talk, I paid only a brief visit to Mr. Lindstrom's house. He was sound asleep but had thrown off the coverlet and was clutching his pillow, as if for comfort. Poor betrayed, abandoned Mr. Lindstrom!

How lucky it is, I thought, as I gazed lovingly down upon him, that the master bedroom should be at the back of the house, and that the window near the bed should be so close to a very convenient tree. Since the rear windows faced into dense woods, Mr. Lindstrom (or more probably, the heartless Mrs. Lindstrom) had felt it was unnecessary to use any but thin net curtains on the bedroom window. Owl eyesight is far superior to human vision, just as our sense of hearing far surpasses yours. I could see him perfectly clearly.

The moon was nearly full. Fat and white and terribly bright, it lit the wintry world about me with a cold silvery light, throwing knife-edged shadows behind every stick and stone. The bird feeder creaked gently in the wind, and an iced-over birdbath glittered dimly in the moon's beams. I regarded these objects with pleasure. They were intended for the use of songbirds and suchlike silly beasts, but they warmed my heart all the same. We had something in common after all: we were both interested in birds!

My sensitive ears detected below me the shrill bickering of a pair of mice, foolishly abroad in the night. Mice, as you may know, are quarrelsome, peevish animals in their private lives, always squeaking out their discontents for all the world to hear. It makes them very easy to catch. Beside me the gray skeleton fingers of the maple tree scraped out a melancholy tune, reminding me that winter is the time of famine and that I had need of something to put weight on my underfed frame. I pounced.

No mouse ever tasted sweeter. It could be, I thought, as I swallowed the morsel whole (headfirst is best), that this very mouse had entered Mr. Lindstrom's house, had fed upon his bread and cheese, had nibbled on his soap and candles. Here was communion indeed! I sat motionless outside his window, digesting reverently.

Then, my eyes and brain filled with his image and my stomach (possibly) filled with bits and scrapings of his intimate possessions, I flew off into the chill night. The pursuit of love must, after all, sometimes give way to the pursuit of a meal.

• • •

"What are you looking at? What do you see?"

"The window."

"And why does that make you look so unhappy?"

Windows did worry him. How thin they were, and how brittle! The barrier between danger and security was narrower than the thickness of his little finger. The glass held back the bright winter sky, kept him cocooned in a warm bubble of air. If he touched the glass he could feel the cold air rushing by just a few millimeters away from his fingertips.

In movies he watched on the television in the lounge people sometimes fell, or were pushed, through windows like this. The glass would erupt outward in millions of tiny fragments. The victim always dropped in exquisite slow motion, soundlessly, like a falling snowflake.

In this room, this building, he was safe, but the windows were so fragile, so easily punctured. Like the television, they teased him with visions of a perilous world he must not enter. He was not tempted by the world the television offered, but the view from the windows, the high curved cup of sky fringed by forest, called to him treacherously.

"What are you thinking? You seem sad."

Words. They always wanted words and were so pleased with themselves when they succeeded in winning one or two from him. It was as though they thought that words were more real, more solid, than he was himself. Perhaps they were right.

"Can we talk about the biting? I understand you hurt yourself again. You were asleep?"

The dreams. *I could be bounded in a nutshell and count myself a king of infinite space, were it not that I have bad dreams.* For a moment he could not trace the quotation to its source. Then he remembered. William Shakespeare, *Hamlet*.

I may be mad, but at least I'm well read.

He laughed silently, the muscles of his face motionless.

A nutshell. Yes, this place was his nutshell, and he would willingly be bound up in it, and by it, were it not for his dreams.

He closed his eyes. He was the man falling, so slowly, so peacefully, through the window. His spine arched, his arms outstretched. The wind streaked through his fingers like flags.

Terrible dreams, of blood and fear and death, yet they were the only real happiness he had ever known.

"Very well. We'll talk later. Your mother sent you more books. I believe they have been taken to your room."

Three

"You've got a crush on Mr. Lindstrom, haven't you?"

Startled, I looked up. For a moment I thought that last night's full moon had descended from the heavens to demand an explanation of my emotional state. But no, the round, moony face belonged to Dawn Mitchell, the girl who lived in Hillcrest Estates, she who had so helpfully volunteered Mr. Lindstrom's address as well as information on his marital status.

"I beg your pardon? A what?" I said, a little stiffly.

"A crush . . . you know, a pash, a fave. C'mon, Owl, you're weird and all, but you're not so weird you don't know plain English. You've got the hots for old Lindstrom. Right?"

"That is not the way I would describe my feelings for our mutual science teacher, no," I said.

"So, okay, maybe it's not the way *you'd* say it, but anybody else would."

I was silent for a moment, considering what this implied.

"*Do* other people say so?"

"No." Dawn snorted and snuffled with amusement. "They think you're trying to put a hex on him." This was so comic she had to clutch at herself in order to contain her delight. "They think," she giggled, "that you hate his guts. They're all waiting for him to be found at the bottom of a flight of stairs with a broken neck and a look of *horror* on his face." She demonstrated, lolling her head to one side at an unnatural angle, thrusting her tongue out, and bugging her eyes at me.

"Actually, I thought so too, at first," Dawn admitted. "The way you stare at him, like you wanna just eat him right up . . . whew! It's really intense." She studied me. "You've got it bad, don't you?" she asked, a trace of sympathy coloring her voice.

I was just about to deliver myself of a crushing remark in return, when I stopped to reconsider. Little as I cared for Dawn's tone, I reflected that this might be her idea of a friendly opening. What I needed, today of all days, was an ally in science class.

I had given much thought to what I should do about this blood-type lab scheduled for today. Before setting out for school I pricked my finger and experimented with food coloring. The black became not one shade redder. Anyway, what was the point? My blood would never have reacted normally to the tests.

I returned Dawn's openly curious gaze. She looked as

though she had plenty of good, red blood in her. She was as pink as a peony.

Pretending illness or any of the other schemes I had had in mind was no more than a temporary solution. I would be expected to make up the lab eventually.

"Have you got an unusual blood type?" I asked.

"Huh?"

I saw that I was moving too quickly. Dawn's mind was on romance, while mine was on blood samples.

"Sorry. I was thinking of the science lab today."

"Oh! No, I don't think so." Dawn seemed reluctant to let go of the more fascinating topic of my love life, but after a brief struggle she accepted the change of subject gracefully. With her frank and forthright approach to delicate matters, she probably considered a change of subject preferable to a punch in the nose. "No, I think I'm just boring old O pos."

Suddenly inspired, I said, "Are you scared of doing that blood thing today?"

"Scared? Of course not. It's just a little prick. Sort of disgusting squeezing it out I guess, but it's no big deal. Why?"

"Oh, it gives me the cold horrors," I said, and gave a convincing shudder. I am not a chatty person as a rule, but in this emergency I forced myself to gush a little. "I know it's stupid of me, but I just can't stand the thought of it. I hate the sight of blood, especially my own."

Dawn shrugged. "Then don't do it."

"We *have* to do it," I said a little irritably. "I'm afraid I'll faint," I added pathetically. Perhaps I was overdoing it. Dawn looked suddenly interested, as though this was an event she wouldn't want to miss. After a moment's indecision, however, she proved that she owned a better nature.

"Be my lab partner," she offered. "I'll give you a drop of blood."

"Oh, would you?"

"Sure." She looked at me again. "You know, it's funny. I'd never have thought you'd go faint at the sight of a whole swimming pool full of blood, let alone one measly little drop. Shows I'm not such a good judge of character as I thought."

I didn't answer. A whole swimming pool of blood seemed a bit excessive, but allowing for a little exaggeration on her part, she was perfectly right. Why anyone should faint at the sight of blood, I cannot imagine. People can be very odd.

However, Dawn seemed satisfied, and when we met in science class the deception came off quite neatly. My darling was moving about the opposite end of the room casting kindly glances over students' shoulders—

I break off here because I realize that I have never given a proper description of Mr. Lindstrom. It seems amazing that when you read the words "Mr. Lindstrom," you do not immediately see him before you as I do.

I have spoken of his receding hairline and his age (it was Dawn who told me he was forty; she seems to collect this sort of information). He is not very tall—about five feet six—and thickening slightly at the waist. How unromantic this sounds! How can I make you understand? Well, perhaps I can't. It is one of the Mysteries.

What do I care if he is not what the world would call handsome? Neither am I what the world would call pretty, so we are well suited. His voice, I think, is what first moved me. A deep husky rumble, it trembles within my bone and muscle long after he is silent. Yes, it is his voice that binds me to him.

For the rest, he has thick sandy hair and pale gray eyes, clever hands, and a humorous mouth. He is well liked, I believe, by his students and fellow teachers.

Dawn punctured her index finger and without so much as a guilty glance around her, casually dabbed her finger on my slides and then her own.

I, watching with some admiration and, thinking to repay her kindness, commented, "You seem to have excellent nerves for carrying out this sort of exploit. What kind of career did you have in mind for your future?"

Dawn gave a shout of laughter so loud it turned Mr.

Lindstrom's gaze in our direction. He frowned, and I cringed inwardly.

"What, you think I should go into crime in a big way? Bank jobs, that sort of thing?"

"Of course not. I meant a career on the other side of the fence, naturally."

"A spy for the CIA!" Dawn suggested, her eyes dancing. "Sure! Why not?" She nudged me with her elbow cozily. "Owl, you're okay. I like you," she said, as though conferring some great honor. "Here, have a Ding Dong."

I naturally refused this sticky pastry with thanks. "That's right," she said, nodding her head. "You don't eat, do you? Good trick if you can manage it." She nodded ruefully at her waistline.

I did not reply, because Mr. Lindstrom, who had somehow managed to approach us without my being aware, was at my side. I, who had thought I could distinguish his slightest movement from rooms away, felt his jacket hem brush my arm and almost shrugged it off as an annoyance. Then his own distinctive scent caught at my nostrils. I froze, like a rabbit that feels the shadow of an owl slide down its spine.

"So, Dawn, Owl, you're a team this time, eh?" he inquired, sounding as though he thought we made an odd couple.

Too shaken to even nod agreement, I let Dawn respond.

"Oh, hi, Mr. Lindstrom," Dawn said. "Yeah, sure." She glanced at me, and her eyes lit up with mischief. "Hey, Mr. Lindstrom, don't you think Owl looks pretty today?"

"Owl always looks pretty," said Mr. Lindstrom lightly. "A little pale, maybe. Let's see your blood sample, Owl." He held a slide up to the light, pretending to admire the color. "Red as a rose in June," he said, handing it back to me. "I must admit it's a relief to see that. I've sometimes wondered if Owl had fairy blood in her veins." And, patting my shoulder, he moved on.

Dawn's eyes narrowed and she looked at me thoughtfully. Her suspicions, whatever they might be, did not concern me at the moment. There was a thrumming of my black "fairy" blood in my ears, so that the babble of the science lab was nearly silenced, and Dawn's round face looked as small and faraway as a penny at the bottom of a well.

"Are you going to faint?" demanded a teeny, tiny voice.

"Of course not," I started to say, and I wasn't, either. Just a momentary giddiness from the touch of his hand. But Dawn was not to be cheated of drama.

"Catch her, Mr. Lindstrom!" Dawn shrilled.

And then, of course, I did faint.

I fainted! Of all the stupid, idiotic times to faint. My darling, my own, my sweet, held me in his arms, and I missed it! Of course, if I hadn't fainted he would not have been holding me in his arms. If only I had *pretended* to faint, I could have enjoyed it.

When I came to, I was still sitting in my chair. Mr. Lindstrom was squatting beside me with one arm around my shoulder while with the other he motioned the crowd of morbidly curious students away.

"Back to your seats, everybody. This happens every year. Nothing to get excited about."

Oh, Mr. Lindstrom, how can you say so?

"She *said* she'd faint if she had to do it!" Dawn squawked hysterically.

"Owl." Mr. Lindstrom was reproachful. "You should have told me." He lowered his voice, speaking only to me. "With most of these idiots, I'd have told 'em not to damage the linoleum when they hit the floor, but Owl, I'd have listened to you." He made a wry face. "You talk so rarely I have to listen when you do say something." He smiled at me. "Don't worry. They'll all forget about it in a day or two."

He thought I was embarrassed. I was in heaven. I could not meet his eyes but looked instead at his hand, where it curved around my arm. Tiny golden hairs grew on the backs of the bottom joints of his fingers, like delicate stalks of wheat. Beneath the prevailing aromas of Lifebuoy and Mennen, I easily detected his own dear Mr. Lindstrom smell. I breathed in. I could not speak.

34

"How are you feeling? Maybe you'd better go to the nurse. You look a little shell-shocked still."

I shook my head no. Not unless I could manage it so he would carry me. I considered fainting again. No. That might lead to doctors or to interference from the school into my home life. He removed his arm and stood up. A sense of desolation settled upon me, and I shivered a little. He hesitated a moment, watching me anxiously. "Sure?"

I nodded, more vigorously. *Say* something, I urged myself. "I'm fine, Mr. Lindstrom," I said in marvelously calm tones. "I'm sorry to have worried you."

"All right, then." He smiled, a warm, intimate smile, just between us. My heart thumped unpleasantly against my ribs, and I moaned softly. Unheeding, he walked away.

Dawn immediately moved in.

"If I didn't see the way your eyeballs rolled up into your head just before you keeled over, I'da said you planned the whole thing," she murmured. "Except"—she cocked her head at me—"I don't know. You're hard to figure, Owl, the hardest person to figure I ever met. The way you said that just now, so prim and prissy and polite, maybe you don't have a crush on Mr. Lindstrom. Maybe you *are* gonna put a spell on him. Turn him into a frog before midterms, will ya?"

After the fainting incident, Dawn seemed to lose interest in my affairs, at least temporarily, and began chattering about her own. Being involved in a lengthy conversation with someone not of my family was quite new to me. While Dawn did nearly all the talking, she seemed to expect some response other than my silent attention. This was not entirely easy, as she spoke of many things new to my experience, and much of her slang puzzled me.

While this, and the nervous tension I felt at the physical closeness of another human being, were something of a strain, I was surprised to discover within myself some slight stirrings of pleasure in this odd girl's company. Having never possessed a friend in my life (excepting always my parents), I found myself wondering what that experience might be like.

We owls make devoted, 'til-death-do-us-part mates, but we are otherwise solitary creatures. As predators defending a territory, it is not surprising that we do not often engage in friendships.

I am, however, half human, a species well known for a terrifyingly efficient social structure. When creatures possessing large brains, upright posture, and opposable thumbs decide to bury their differences and cooperate with one another, all nature trembles.

Dawn appeared to take our future cooperation as lab partners for granted and was presently favoring me with intimate details about her parents' marriage, her uncle's drinking habits, and a blow-by-blow account of a quarrel between her brother and herself.

". . . and when I said it was *my* cupcake, my mom just said I was too fat anyway, so El Stinko"—this appears to refer to her brother, rather an unusual name, I thought—"ate it even though I *told* him I'd already licked it."

Dawn's family seems to exist in a state of constant turmoil and strife. As I listened, my own peaceful, loving family became doubly dear to me by contrast. In this charitable mood, I could not help but feel that it might be proper—surely it would be generous—to forgive my father for his attitude toward Mr. Lindstrom. When I parted from Dawn I felt that her influence had done me no harm but rather some actual good.

Four

THERE IS ANOTHER OWL in the wood behind Mr. Lindstrom's house. His presence, and that of another intruder, make me very uneasy.

I don't mean the married screech owl couple that live in the old oak tree a quarter of a mile away. I have been aware of them ever since I took to watching Mr. Lindstrom. The male threatens me whenever we happen to meet, but without much enthusiasm. Mr. Lindstrom's house is on the outer boundary of their territory, and besides, other owls tend to avoid me, sensing something alien. Add to this the fact that I outweigh the little screech owl by about two to one, and it becomes clear why his threats are halfhearted.

No, the stranger is a young, unmarried male owl of my own species (a barn owl), who seems to have about as much sense as an unhatched egg. His behavior, I hasten to add, does not in any way resemble courtship. True, the breeding season is fast approaching, but I know the signs. Young as I am, I was once approached by a gentleman with nesting on his mind.

I admit that at the time I thought the old fellow had

gone mad. Thinking things over later, I realized that he was not mad, only mistaken. A widower, he was confused by the fact that, even though I was apparently a child too young for marriage, I had flown the woods about my parents' home ever since he was a boy himself. Looking for a mate to replace his deceased wife, he presented me with a dead frog and made certain suggestions that, in my innocence, I did not at all understand. He then began to dance in a most ridiculous and undignified way, shuffling about on the branch we shared, looking like a justice of the Supreme Court performing a striptease. It was very embarrassing. I had no idea how to handle the situation, so I simply flew away. I never saw him again.

I should perhaps explain that owls in the wild live only about three to five years, if they make it to adulthood at all. My life as an owl, however, has been tied to the timetable of human development. Until six years of age, in my owl form I was nothing but a peeping bundle of white fuzz, totally dependent upon my parents as a nest-bound infant. Mother and Father fed me by setting traps in and around our house.

At six I lost my baby down and grew adult plumage; at eight I learned to fly. What an excitement that made in our quiet lives! My poor dear parents, how sad it is that they can never experience the joys of free flight. When I think of this, I realize that I am privileged indeed.

Since then I have led the life of a juvenile. Unlike many juveniles, I possess a territory of my own, simply because I have lived in the area so long.

I am not now quite of marriageable age but close enough that an unmarried male might take some interest in me. I therefore felt somewhat self-conscious when, instead of either fleeing from me or attacking me, as I might have expected a strange owl to do, this new one started up a conversation of sorts.

"Who," he said, rather hesitantly.

"Who who?" I asked, not unreasonably.

Owl faces are not very expressive, but his eyes widened with what I took to be surprise, as though I had said something shocking.

"Who," he repeated, fixing me with a glittering, intense eye. He leaned forward. He looked as though he might be about to start foaming at the beak and shouting out slogans about the end of the world. "*Who*," he added for good measure.

"What are we talking about?" I asked, attempting to inject a little common sense into what was becoming a rather tense dialogue.

"Oh hell," he said, or words to that effect, and flew clumsily away.

It was very odd. I have seen him once or twice, always near Mr. Lindstrom's house, but ever since that time he turns his head away when he sees me and flies off, muttering. I don't like it. He seems mentally unbalanced. I would drive him away, but I feel it is not really fitting since it is not my territory.

Speaking of strangers haunting the woods behind Mr. Lindstrom's house, there is a human intruder as well. This I find even more disquieting. An insane owl might be a danger to me, but the boy in the woods might be a danger to Mr. Lindstrom.

It certainly seems likely that he is a danger to Mr. Lindstrom's house and possessions. I have seen him several times peering in through Mr. Lindstrom's rear windows, and I am deeply suspicious of his intentions. You will remind me, perhaps, that I myself have spent considerable amounts of time peering through those same windows (only one floor up). I did so, as you know quite well, for love of Mr. Lindstrom. I flatly refuse to believe it is affection looking out of those big greedy black eyes as the boy stares into the darkness of Mr. Lindstrom's family room.

He has a disagreeable look, this boy. My guess is that he is about my age or slightly older, but shorter and smaller than I. The expression in his eyes, though, might belong to a man of forty, assuming that those forty years had been both long and bitter. Sinister dark eyes are set above a thin bony beak of a nose and a tiny slit of a mouth. He looks decidedly abnormal.

I am torn. My nightly vigil outside my love's window has of late become fairly brief, in response to my mother's wishes. After all, it seems a sensible request. Pining away like the young lady in Shakespeare who never told her love but "sat like patience on a monument, smiling at grief," sounds romantic, but I suspect the reality of winter starvation might be a little less elegant and a good deal more uncomfortable.

Still, with this new menace on the scene, this wicked-eyed boy prowling and slinking around the edges of my darling's slumber, I feel very uncomfortable about deserting him merely to feed myself. For the present I dare do nothing to draw attention, but if I should see the evil boy breaking or entering, I promise you he will learn the grip of my talons.

I will try for larger prey to stave off my hunger, and so be free to watch by the window longer. I have sometimes caught fat rabbits hopping in the moonlight around our frozen vegetable garden. Rabbits do not possess any great intellect, I fear. The garden of a wereowl at midnight makes a perilous salad bar.

"Hey, Owl," a voice hailed me, as twelve hours later I made my solitary way to a cafeteria table. The voice and the table both belonged, I discovered, to Dawn. She sat alone, almost hidden from view behind a lunch tray piled high with plastic-encased goodies from the snack table.

My stomach groaned in envy at the sight, even of this starchy, sticky fare. The fat rabbits had learned wisdom, it seemed. No stooping, hunched forms had revealed themselves to me last night browsing among the frigid Brussels sprouts, and my empty innards clanged like a gong.

"I was thinking," Dawn said, as I approached her table. "Here, siddown." She motioned at the place opposite her. "Have you ever tried makeup?"

"I beg your pardon?"

"Makeup, Owl. Cosmetics, war paint—you know. Sometimes I feel like I'm talking Swahili with you. I mean, the only thing that's really out-and-out bizarre about you is your skin color. Those big eyes are freaky, sure, but they could be a real asset, you know? Kind of hypnotic and compelling, like." She picked up a package of cookies and began an assault on the tough plastic with her teeth.

In the space underneath the cookies' resting place a fat sausage lolling in a bun revealed itself. I stared at this object, fascinated. Would it be possible, I asked myself, to pretend that it was something edible—a stunted, over-weight garter snake, for instance—and, with eyes shut, gobble it down so quickly that the taste would not linger? Possibly. The thing was made of processed pig flesh rather than dog meat as the name "hot dog" implied. It stank of factories and chemicals, but still, my stomach argued, one must not be narrow-minded. How much difference could one sausage make?

". . . You could come over to my house," Dawn was saying. "I've got drawers and drawers of makeup. My mother sells the stuff."

My eyes narrowed as I withdrew from consideration of the hot dog and looked warily at Dawn. Go over to her house? Why on earth would she want me to do that? Was she, I wondered uncomfortably, aware of my designs upon her hot dog and considering ways and means of revenge?

I shook my head to clear it. Don't be so foolish, I commanded myself. You are thinking as an owl, not a human. Teenage girls often invite each other over to their homes. It is a gesture of friendship.

"Well," Dawn said coldly, "sorry I asked. I just thought I'd try to help out."

She had, I saw, taken my head shake as a refusal.

"You misunderstand me," I said quickly, and before I knew it, had agreed to spend an hour with her at her home that very afternoon, applying colored creams to my skin. The oddity and intimacy of this image so rattled me that I could barely reply to the stream of cozy chatter she now directed my way. Luckily, it appeared not to be necessary to do much more than nod or shake my head at intervals.

My visit to Dawn's house in Hillcrest Estates was indeed a strange and memorable adventure. I had to ride in a school bus to get there. I tried to convince Dawn to walk. She could not believe I meant it, though my sincerity must have been obvious.

"Are you crazy? It's four miles to my house. We'd die of exhaustion."

In vain I tried to convince her that four miles was hardly any distance at all. "It is *too*," she responded, with more energy than I would have believed she possessed. "You're nuts, Owl. It'd take us years. I never walked even half a mile in my life."

I, on the other hand, had never ridden in any motorized vehicle in *my* life. Most unwillingly I approached the stinking orange monsters lined up outside the school and prepared to be swallowed whole. In my panic I wondered if I might not unintentionally shift from human to owl shape before all these onlooking eyes to escape this unexpected danger. Had I been in owl form, I know my bill would've been clacking like a choir of castanets.

It was just as well that I was fasting when I rode that school bus. On a full stomach I fear I would have disgraced myself. It took a firm push from Dawn's large hand in the small of my back to persuade me to climb those ominous black steps. She propelled me down the aisle and to a seat thankfully close to the rear door. We then had to wait an eternity until the bus filled up, and the driver (a bad-tempered, muscular woman of about sixty) agreed to set the thing in motion. I begged the woman several times to have done with all this hanging about and get a move on, but she refused to stir a muscle until the mystic hour of 2:36.

"Keep yer hair on, kid," was the advice she offered.

Dawn was fascinated by my reactions. "Gee, you're really scared, aren't you?" She eyed me with scientific detachment, like the good Doctor Frankenstein observing the effects of a couple of thousand volts of electricity on his monster's reflexes.

"Haven't you ever ridden on a school bus before?" she asked.

"No," I gritted through clenched teeth. The bus had at last lurched forward, growling hideously all the while. Every instinct protested my situation: the narrow, sweating, stinking box crammed to bursting with humanity, all sliding and jostling against each other. Dawn's arm brushed mine as we rounded a sharp curve and I emitted a little high-pitched shriek.

"Wow, weird." Dawn watched me closely for all four endless, rattling, jerking miles to her house to avoid missing, I suppose, any of the finer shades of terror I might be exhibiting.

At last, after nearly every other soul had been released

from the grip of this mobile home of the damned, we arrived. Dawn jabbed me with her elbow to indicate that this was our stop, and I released my grip on the seat back before me and staggered toward freedom.

Once outside I collapsed onto a convenient low wall, which formed a part of the entrance to Hillcrest Estates. With one last blast of carbon monoxide (aimed, I will swear, straight at me) the vile contraption roared away down the hill.

"Hey, how're you gonna get home?" Dawn asked. "You can call your mom from our house. Maybe she can pick you up."

I shook my head. "No telephone, no automobile," I explained tersely, still concentrating upon getting some untainted oxygen into my lungs.

"What!"

"I will walk," I lied. Actually, of course, I intended to fly. If you are one of those who foolishly believe that owls cannot see during the day, prepare to learn otherwise. We fly at night simply because our eyesight is so superb that we can easily see in light that leaves others groping helplessly about, bumping their shins on the furniture. With this obvious advantage there is little reason to fly during the daylight hours, especially since it is during the day that humans like to relieve their aggressive impulses by letting off firearms into the air.

"Oh no," said Dawn, clearly shocked. "I can't let you do that. Wait until my mother gets home and she'll drive you."

"No!" I said with some violence, imagining myself cooped up in yet another, and smaller, vehicle. "That is, thank you very much, Dawn, but I would prefer to walk. Really."

"Well," said Dawn dubiously, "suit yourself. I live down this way. Mr. Lindstrom's house is over that-away."

I knew this, of course, but having never been here in human form I was surprised at the difference in perspective. Earthbound structures can never look as impressive to a sky creature as they do to those who must crawl over the ground always looking up and never down.

While the acres of housing developments that have sprung up around our town are depressing and threatening enough from the air, I had never before felt so surrounded by the results of purposeful human activity. The houses, with their clean modern lines, each set in a perfectly manicured quarter of an acre, each with a barbecue grill huddled, snowcapped and forlorn, under its eaves, oppressed me. My own shabby home in my own shabby neighborhood was suggestive of human frailty and the eventual triumph of time and nature over the best efforts of human beings. These houses seemed not to believe in death or decay. What, I wondered, would it be like to have grown up in this neighborhood, instead of in my own dearly beloved home, with my own dear parents?

With a shock it occurred to me—would Mr. Lindstrom expect me to live here with him, in the event of our marriage? No, no, I could not believe it of him. It was no doubt his wife who had picked that house, this neighborhood. Of his own will he would choose the seedy grandeur of a mansion on Muldaur Street in town, or perhaps a lonely farmhouse a few miles out into the country.

Cheered by this reflection, I realized that Dawn was looking at me expectantly, waiting for a response. Quickly I reviewed her last words in my mind. ". . . But I don't mind walking around the long way so we can go by his house," she had just said.

"If you like," I agreed. Mr. Lindstrom was unlikely to be there, as he was probably still grading papers at school. Still, since she was so kind to suggest it, I was always glad to visit even this, his temporary outer shell.

Dawn seemed disappointed at my attitude. "I don't know about you, Owl, I just don't know. Are you crackers about the guy or not?"

As she seemed to expect no answer, I gave her none. She stared, considering me as though I were a locked steel vault that she suspected of concealing an entire case of Twinkies.

Five

"THIS'S HIS HOUSE. See, it says Lindstrom on the mailbox. He's given me a ride to school once or twice when I missed the bus. I'd rather've stayed home, but who's gonna argue with a teacher?"

I studied the house from the street. It kept its secret well. Almost anyone might have lived there. How strange that this most ordinary of houses should belong to my love.

"Uh-hum," I said.

"I never knew the son," she said casually.

I turned to stare at her. The son? What son?

"You don't know about the son, do you?" Dawn demanded triumphantly. "Well, I almost forgot about him, myself. I've never even seen him. He goes to a private school, one of those sleep-away ones. My mother says she can't imagine how two teachers could afford it."

I considered this new complication. Well, it wasn't so bad. He was at that school. Holidays or vacations he would probably mostly spend with his mother. Still, we would have to see him sometimes. How old would he be, I wondered? Six, seven? Or even nine or ten? I wriggled uncomfortably at the thought of a ten-year-old stepson. But no, he was much more likely to be seven: half my age.

"My mother did say she heard"—Dawn stole a cautious look at me—"that it was a special school."

"Oh?" I said, not really interested.

"Actually, I wouldn't pay any attention to anything my mother says," Dawn said frankly. "She's a terrible gossip. Well, this is my house. C'mon in. My horrible brother is at his horrible friend's house, so we've got the place to ourselves."

Dawn's house was nice enough inside, I suppose, if you like all that furniture and that glaring sunlight pouring in at the windows. To my taste it seemed awfully cluttered. There was an armchair *and* a sofa in the living room, not to mention two little end tables, a coffee table, and a hassock. All this, jammed into a room not one third the size of our back parlor. You couldn't walk ten feet in any direction without bumping into a piece of overstuffed furniture.

Owls are not house-proud. The almost obsessive tidiness of this room made me uneasy. A few rotting branches or some old leaves would have made the place look a lot homier, in my opinion. To each his own, I suppose.

Still, I paid little attention to this. The moment I entered the house I sensed prey, and if you will recall the hollow condition of my innards, you will understand my emotions.

Birds in general have a poor sense of smell. Odors tend to sink to the ground rather than hover in the air, so smell is less important to us than to earth-dwellers. But owls can smell much better than most birds, and humans can smell quite well, though they rarely trouble to use the talent. At the moment, I smelled a rat. Or some sort of rodent, anyway. I tasted the air. It came from upstairs.

"Oh, Owl, I just have to have a snack when I get home from school. Do you want anything?"

I most certainly did. I wanted the source of that enticing aroma.

"Well, look. I'll bring some stuff upstairs, and if you see anything you like, just take it," she said. How kind, I thought. If only I can flush it out from its hiding place without her seeing it too. Perhaps I could ask to go upstairs to her room and wait for her?

Dawn had the refrigerator door open and was shoveling armloads of foodstuffs onto a tray. She straightened. "Here, Owl, you take the tray. I gotta heat some junk up in the microwave."

I took the heavily laden tray and began to open my mouth to ask the way to her room when her eyes focused on an unopened box of cookies on my tray.

"Oooh!" she shrieked in delight. "Mint cookies! My favorite. I thought they were just the plain old ordinary ones. Wait! Wait! Don't move. I've got to have one right now!" Feverishly, she ripped the wrappings off the box and grabbed three. "Have one," she urged through a mouthful of crumbs.

"No, thank you." The fumes of chocolate and mint now entirely obscured the faint but delightful odor of small mammal.

Beeeeeeeeeeeep!

I screamed and nearly dropped the tray.

"Geez, Owl, you sure are jumpy. It's just the micro-wave."

I have seen microwaves in magazines before. I had recognized it, along with the refrigerator and electric range and oven. I even understood its purpose. I just didn't expect it to make that infernal noise. We owls have very sensitive ears.

"Of course," I said with dignity.

"Okay, first room on the left upstairs. Here, I'll show you."

Dawn preceded me up the carpeted stairs, leading me nearer and nearer to the rodent. I heard tiny rustling sounds, as of a little animal nestling down among straw. How was I going to capture and eat the creature without Dawn's knowledge?

Come to that, how had the little thing's presence escaped Dawn's notice? If I could smell it, surely Dawn must.

I saw it at once. It huddled in the corner of a large glass box on Dawn's desk. Perhaps it had fallen in and was unable to escape. Queer, but I could not decide exactly what manner of beast it was. Not a mouse or a rat or a vole. Not a shrew or a squirrel . . .

"Have you ever had a hamster?" asked Dawn, bending over the box.

Having no idea of what a hamster might be, I did not immediately answer, but watched her, puzzled, as she removed it and held it out for my inspection.

You, of course, will know what it was. You no doubt are amused by my stupidity. But really, tell me, how was I to know? As she held out the fat little twitching body on the palm of her hand, I could only imagine that, amazing as it seemed, she had guessed my desires and was giving me my after-school snack.

"No, but I've had mice," I assured her, preparing to take her offering, my hands trembling, I must confess, with greed, "and rats and—"

"Ooooh, rats! I know lots of people keep them as pets, but I just never liked the look of those tails."

Pets! I jerked back my hands. A positive Niagara of saliva flooded my mouth, and I stepped back to remove myself from temptation. I have been carefully raised.

Hungry as I was I could not be guilty of such a violation of proper conduct as to eat my hostess's pet.

"Don't you want to hold him?"

I shook my head silently, unable to reply.

"Isn't he *sweet?*"

I agreed, untruthfully. It wouldn't taste sweet, no. It would be tender, though, and juicy. I sighed.

The hamster, as she called it, was still partly asleep. With its eyelids barely open it looked even more half-witted than is usual with this sort of creature.

"Here, pet him," Dawn insisted. "He's really friendly." She grabbed my index finger and ran it along the furry spine. The silly animal did not even react. It appeared to be trying, against heavy odds, to go back to sleep again.

Apparently satisfied that I had paid my respects to her pet, she put the little morsel back into its cage and began rummaging in a drawer.

"Lessee, here's a buncha goop. My mom brings all this junk home and gives it to me. I could start up a beauty salon with just what I got in my room. There's tons more in the bathroom."

Out of one drawer she took a hefty stack of teenage magazines and plopped them down in front of me. To distract my attention from my rumbling tummy, I took one up and leafed through it.

"There's lotsa stuff about makeup in here. I think

there was something a couple of months ago about unusual skin tones." Dawn's voice became muffled as she bit into a banana.

I found articles on makeup in my magazine as well. Also clothing styles, an article on dating tips, a short story about a girl who'd had a fight with her best friend, advice columns, and advertisements.

One advertisement near the back offered to supply "a guy all your own" for quite a modest fee. I skimmed through it, idly wondering how the company managed to get around the Thirteenth Amendment of the Constitution prohibiting slavery and involuntary servitude. A closer reading revealed that an actual flesh-and-blood male would not be delivered to your door, only a book of instructions on how to attract one. Also available was a textbook on kissing techniques.

Interesting. I had not considered the technical aspects of the matter before. Perhaps when the supreme moment arrived I would be unable to perform adequately. How depressing; here was yet something else to worry about.

"Here it is!" Dawn's cry broke into my musing. "I found it. Okay now, you're a brunette, with . . . well it's not exactly olive skin or. . . . None of these seem quite right. You don't have any of these shades of black or brown skin. You've got pale gray skin. It's not on the chart. So forget that. What we do is try to find the color closest to yours. Hmmm. This could be difficult. Here, c'mon, Owl, help."

I do not myself believe that the color we eventually selected was very close to my own. It was quite true, as Dawn said, that the major cosmetic companies of America seemed to be unprepared for a complexion like mine. Dawn pinned my hair back (exclaiming at its softness) and began to slather the cool lotion onto my face.

She had positioned me in such a way that I could not avoid looking at the hamster. Before leaving him to his own devices, she had dumped a handful of dried food pellets into his cage. This had awakened him from his slumber, and he was methodically placing them one by one into his mouth. *Five, six, seven* . . . for want of anything better to do, I counted them. At number ten, I sat up and began to regard him with some concern. I've seen mice carry seed in their mouths, but this was ridiculous. *Thirteen, fourteen, fifteen* . . . the animal was beginning to look quite deformed. Huge bulges formed all around his neck. My eyes widened. Twenty-three food pellets disappeared into him, or rather they did not disappear but bulged out the skin around his head and shoulders in a most distressing way.

At this point he apparently judged himself well stocked and waddled toward an upright tube in the middle of his cage. Obviously he intended to squash himself into that tube and climb up to a little apartment at the top. A foolish hope! He seemed to agree, for he turned back. It was, however, only to shove an inch-long length of carrot in after the food pellets.

He now looked like a small, furry, hammerhead shark. He returned to his assault on the tube. By dint of much pushing and squeezing, he actually managed to shoehorn himself in and, incredibly, to negotiate the bend of the tube. On several occasions he was obviously unable to move forward or backward, but, by super-rodent effort, managed to twist into a new position and struggle on, ever upward. When he finally reached the top it was all I could do not to cheer.

He turned around in the tiny room facing the tube, opened his jaws unnaturally wide, and with one paw reached into his mouth to unload his burden. It all fell out, the carrot stub and the twenty-three food pellets—all fell down the tube from whence he had carried them with so much labor.

Seldom have I seen an animal stupider than that hamster.

When he saw what he had done, he simply climbed back down the tube and repeated the entire performance all over again, finishing up by spilling the whole load back down the tube again.

And this is the sort of creature that an intelligent

young woman like Dawn chooses to keep for a "pet." The ways of humanity are indeed strange.

By now Dawn had finished applying foundation to my skin and had moved on to powder and blush. She wanted to put mascara on my eyelashes, but I would not allow it. She agreed, saying that my eyes were quite noticeable enough already.

At about this time the rumblings of my stomach became audible even to Dawn's ears.

"So you do need to eat!" she cried in triumph. "There's a few things left on the tray. Wait! You haven't looked at yourself."

I allowed myself to be led out of the room into a bathroom.

I studied myself curiously in the mirror. I looked rather like a pumpkin, or some other member of the squash family. I could not honestly say I thought it an improvement. When I raised a hand to touch my face the difference in color was glaring. Dawn became defensive.

"I mean, you'd have to do your hands too, and your arms and legs if it was summer. If you went swimming . . ." She trailed off.

"Hmmm," I said noncommittally.

"Have some potato chips," she suggested, changing the subject neatly.

A wave of nausea washed over me. It came, I realized,

from hunger rather than distaste. Perhaps I should see if there was anything I could bear to eat. If I ate I might not be able to fly, but that might also be the result if I did not eat. Just a few small bites probably would not prevent my transformation.

Dawn picked through the scanty leavings on the tray, nibbling thoughtfully as she tried to find something I might like.

"Of course," and her eyes lit up at the thought, "there's still lots of things in the refrigerator. Let's go see."

"Dawn! I'm home! Have you been eating, Dawn?"

A strange female voice called up the stairs. I deduced, from the personal nature of the question, that this was Dawn's mother, home from her cosmetic-selling labors.

"Hi, Ma," said Dawn. "No-o-o, not a bite, Ma."

My eyes widened at this transparent falsehood. The evidence of Dawn's snacks lay all over the bedroom and bathroom. Dawn shrugged and then grinned at me as her mother responded, apparently satisfied. "Good."

"Hey, Ma, I got a friend here."

"Oh? Just a minute. I'll be right up."

"No, that's okay, we were just about to come down and see if we could find something for her to eat. She's hungry."

Mrs. Mitchell shouted something inaudible from a distant part of the house. Dawn pulled a white plastic garbage bag out of a drawer in her bedroom. She quickly scraped the litter of packaging material into piles, shoved the piles into the bag and the bag into her closet.

"My mother can never figure out why we get ants," Dawn remarked innocently as we walked downstairs.

"This is Owl, Ma. Owl Tycho," Dawn shouted.

Mrs. Mitchell materialized out of nowhere. "Owl Tycho? You are? *Really?*"

Mrs. Mitchell did not look much like Dawn. They both had the same pink skin and yellow hair, but otherwise they presented an entirely different image. Mrs. Mitchell was thin to the point of discomfort. She looked like a starved cow. She was tall, with large bones that protruded knobbily at her joints. Her makeup, while more skillfully applied than mine, was still not entirely convincing. Surely it is not natural for a healthy human to possess such sky-blue eyelids.

She looked at me with eager curiosity, her eyes raking up and down my modest frame. I suspected she would have liked to walk around me in a circle, drinking in every detail, but manners prevented her.

"Dawn told me she got you for a lab partner of course, but I had no idea she'd actually get you here for a visit. I didn't think you Tychos were very big on paying calls. Lovely jacket, dear. Victorian, I suppose." She fingered my black satin jacket with the jet beading. "*I* couldn't fit into it, that's for sure. And Dawn—well, you two girls are never going to swap clothes, are you? If you don't mind my saying so, dear, the makeup job is a mistake."

"I did the makeup," Dawn said crossly.

"Honestly, Dawn, you should know better. Whatever for?"

Dawn looked huffy. "She's got a thing for Mr.—for this guy. I was just trying to help out."

Mrs. Mitchell looked instantly alert. "'Mister'? An older man, eh? Watch out, dear, you're playing with fire." She chortled. "One of your teachers, right?"

"Oh, Ma!" Dawn said uneasily, shooting an embarrassed look at me.

"You ought to be safe enough there, anyway. Teachers know better than to get mixed up with female students."

"That's the problem."

Mrs. Mitchell laughed shortly. "Ho! You think that's a problem? You girls don't know what problems are, that's all I can say." She sighed and looked nostalgic. "Not that I don't sympathize. I remember my music teacher the year I was thirteen. I just thought he was the most wonderful thing! Bald, of course, and he had this awful breath, but I would have died for a kind word from him."

She shook her head. "Oh, those teenage years. You know what I would give to have them back again?"

"I don't know, Ma. What would you give to have your teenage years back again?"

"Nothing. Absolutely not one thin dime. In fact, I'd pay anything not to have to live them over again. Worst time of my entire life."

"Well, okay, nobody's gonna force you to drink at the Fountain of Youth."

"Youth is a vastly overrated experience, believe me."

"We believe you, Ma. We're the ones having the experience."

"Not very talkative, your friend, is she?"

"No, Ma, I told you. She never says anything."

"She *can* talk, can't she?"

"Sure she can talk, whaddya think?"

"How do you do, Mrs. Mitchell," I said quickly.

"See?"

"Well, okay, I just wondered. I mean, you can't blame me for wondering."

"So what do we have to eat?"

"You should know, if anybody does," Mrs. Mitchell retorted. I wondered how Dawn explained where all those groceries went to every week. I could only assume that Mrs. Mitchell knew more than Dawn thought she did.

"Did you pick up some Hostess cakes like I asked you?"

"Sure. They're right over by the cookie jar. Dawn? Make sure Owl gets some first, okay?"

Dawn made some answer, but it was hard to understand, with her mouth full of cake.

• • •

"Owl?" Dawn paused in her chewing a few minutes later. Not looking at me, she said in a carefully casual tone, "Of course, we both know she's right. I mean, it's more like a joke than anything else, right? Old Lindstrom dating a kid like you!" She snuck a quick peek at me to check my reaction.

Occupied in investigating the baked goods, I did not immediately respond.

"Hey," she said, irritated, "eat that cupcake or don't eat it. Stop poking at it like that. It isn't poisoned. Look, it's right out of the wrapper. Whaddya think we do? Poison all our guests?"

I took a tiny bite. I could verify the fact that it was directly out of the wrapper. The petrochemical odor of the plastic wrap still clung to it.

"I mean, there's lots of guys, *possible* guys we could shoot for. You're really not that bad-looking, you know? Take Randy Nyquist. I know he's kinda dorky, but he's *possible*. He's into science fiction—he might dig you. Wouldn't you rather have a dork than a dream?"

It wasn't her fault. She had no way of knowing that an owl, once bonded to her mate, cannot be wooed away by the most dashing male of her species, let alone a Randy Nyquist.

"Well, wouldn't you?" Dawn demanded sharply.

I had to smile a little. Poor Dawn. She thought I was being silly and unrealistic. I *knew* she was being silly and unrealistic.

"Oh, shut up, Owl!" Dawn snapped, a bit savagely, into a Suzy Q.

Which was really unfair because I hadn't said a thing.

• • •

There were rats in the walls. He was sure of it.

"There are rats in the walls," he told them. "I can hear them at night."

"Sure," they said, and wrote down his words in a notebook. He gave them few words, and so they treasured them in this way, hoarding them up and munching them over in reports and monthly meetings. Whatever they valued in his words, it was not for the sense of them. No notice was taken. The scratching and thumping continued. A slight smell of rodent began to linger in the corners of certain rooms.

It made him nervous. The rats nibbled and pattered their way into his dreams. Waking, he sometimes felt a gush of rage so sweet that he felt himself almost alive. It frightened him, and then he behaved badly. There was noise, confusion, running feet. People shouted at him.

They tidied away the mess and moved him to another floor, but it did no good—the rats and the dreams pursued him.

"He's got his mean look again. Watch out," the attendants on the new floor warned each other.

He wished he knew where the rats came from, how they got in. He would like to see one.

Yes! he would look.

"Whoo-ee! You see that? I ain't goin' nowhere near him, him lookin' like that."

He would look. But first he must be very good, and do everything that was required of him. Then he would see.

Six

I COULD NOT FLY. I didn't even try transforming into owl shape. Having eaten, though sparingly, of Dawn's baked goods in order to ease my hunger pangs, I knew by the heaviness in my middle that I would never make it off the ground. So I walked home. At least I walked part of the way home, as you will see.

Like Dawn, I am unaccustomed to lengthy walking. About a mile from her house I began to suspect that I was developing a blister on my heel. I limped along a little further, looking for somewhere to sit down and investigate. We owls do not care to sit out in the open during daylight hours. I was walking along beside a large cornfield bordered by woods. When at last I reached the wood, I looked around and found a fairly dry log among hemlock trees, twenty feet off the road.

I was quite correct. A small but painful water-filled sac had formed on my left heel. These boots, made for some long-dead ancestor, had never really fit well, and my last pair of socks had worn to ruins six months ago. Since we could not afford to replace them Mother made a virtue of their absence. She said that socks were unimaginative. Father's undershirts had suffered a similar fate two years ago when the last of them fell to pieces in the wash. "Just a teeny bit vulgar" was what she had called Father's undershirts. After that, Father and I could not mourn for our despised underwear, at least not out loud.

I sighed. My parents would be wondering where I was by now. They know I can take care of myself, but they also know that the world is sometimes a perilous place for one small, solitary owl. The sun was sinking steadily toward the western rim of the world. In the east the pale, eggshell-blue of a fine winter's day had begun to shade into deep azure and violet. Perhaps I could make a pad of dried grasses that would protect my heel enough to allow me to limp home.

A heavy, determined thump startled me. There, six feet in front of me, a crow had landed.

"Aaaw!" he said aggressively. Another crow landed ten feet away. I ignored them. It is not my habit to pay any attention to the behavior of crows.

If you know anything about either owls or crows, you will be aware that there is bad blood between our families. It is not precisely a feud, at least not on our side. We owls do not feel it necessary to dignify the situation by noticing it.

Certainly it is true that owls sometimes eat crow eggs. And why not? You yourself, Reader, no doubt eat chicken eggs on a regular basis. Even so, you might feel that this gives crows the moral right to mob owls. "Mobbing" is the term given to the crows' cowardly habit of ganging up in twos, threes, and even fours, against solitary owls.

Oh, crows aren't the only ones. Sometimes songbirds will flutter around a dozing owl making little cheeping sounds for a short time and then retire, their honor apparently satisfied. We owls regard these "attacks" tolerantly. They usually do it only in breeding time, when we are roosting near their nests. Perfectly understandable.

Crows, on the other hand, are nothing but big bullies. They mob owls year-round, in and out of nesting season, when we're not even near their rotten nests.

Crows are the most notorious egg stealers of all time. For every egg I've ever eaten, these black-hearted pirates standing before me have eaten three. And that even takes into account the differences in our ages. Along with the eggs of practically every other species, they also eat owl eggs and nestlings. But do we pester them in public, spoiling their hunting and making the air hideous with ill-mannered screeching? We do not.

These two crows were naturally rather puzzled about me. I looked like a human, moved like a human, and acted like a human, yet against all reason, an "Owl Alert" was flashing inside their skulls.

To give credit where credit is due, crows are not stupid. While largely indifferent to philosophy, science, and the fine arts, they do possess a certain low cunning. I have heard it said that a crow can read a hunting license at five hundred feet.

I ignored them. Resting my bare foot on the too-tight boot, I leaned forward and began to gather dead grasses, not even looking at them.

"Kschh!" In my shock and outrage I hissed an owl cry. One of the crows had advanced and pecked at my sore foot. She (for it was a female) cawed loudly. The other crow, emboldened, edged nearer and cried out in triumph as though it had been he who had pecked me.

"Go away!" I said. I cast about myself for a weapon. All I could find was a small, light stick. I threw it in her direction. It did not hit her, but it seemed to make her think a bit.

Just as it looked as though she was going to back off, two other crows, summoned by the loud cawing, flew down to us. More hoarse calls sounded off in the wood. With a sinking heart, I realized that I had chosen to rest almost directly under a large crow roost.

Working quickly I cushioned my ankle, and, leaving the laces of my boot undone, limped out of the wood, back into the neighboring field.

Whack! A heavy blow struck the side of my head. The female had hit me with her wing as she flew past. I wrapped my arms tightly around my head and ran for the road hunched over, goblin-like.

The crows struck me again and again, seemingly trying to force me deep into the field, away from the road. If only the margin of that wood had not been their stronghold, the woods themselves would have been the safest place for me; out here in the open I was entirely vulnerable to attack. Thankfully they were not yet using those strong, sharp beaks.

I risked a swift look upward in order to judge the danger. In the triangle of hard blue sky visible between my wrist and arm, too many crows to count wheeled and screamed. At least fifteen, I guessed, before a savage thrust nearly knocked me over.

"Death! Murder! Crow Killer!" they screeched. A black shape appeared suddenly before me, and I ducked again. My upper arms were gripped and violently held.

"Just what in the *hell* are you doing to those birds?" demanded an angry voice.

I opened my eyes and peered out from under my sheltering arms. The black shape was too large to be a crow. Inches away from the toes of my own boots stood a pair of fawn Hush Puppies, size ten, with, I happened to know, a small hole forming in the sole under the left big toe. His sock would be getting damp in the snow. I looked up into Mr. Lindstrom's furious face.

"Out with it, Owl, what were you doing to them?"

So startled was I that I could do nothing but gape at him. I had seen him annoyed before, but never really angry. I learned now to my dismay his look when enraged. I did not much like it, especially as his anger was directed at me, however little I might deserve it. His voice, his set expression, the tension of his attitude, all suggested that he would willingly shake the answer out of me.

"Well?" And he did shake me, a little.

He apparently suddenly realized that he was offering violence to a student, for he let go of me and retreated a step.

"I'm sorry, Owl," he said stiffly. "I shouldn't have done that."

After a moment's silence he seemed to become truly remorseful.

"I really am sorry. It's just that . . ." He looked at me. "Good Lord, what happened to your face? It's all . . . I don't know, orange."

"It's makeup."

"Oh! Oh, I see. I'm sorry. But the birds, Owl. What did you do? Wait, did you pick up a baby that'd fallen out of the nest? That would do it, I guess." His voice was hopeful, imploring me to agree with this ridiculous suggestion. "I shouldn't have jumped on you like that."

I shook my head in silence.

He stared at me without speaking for a moment, then, "No, there wouldn't be any nestlings now, would there, or eggs even? Not for months." His eyes hardened again until they were as bright and cold as the wintry sky above.

"So why were they acting like that, Owl? Crows don't attack people for no reason. What did you do?"

"Nothing."

"Right. I've heard that one before," he said roughly. He was silent a moment, anger visibly swelling his breast. His breath rose in great white clouds of steam over us, like the smoke signals of an advancing war party. My own little puffs of steam waved the white flag in return, signaling frantically: I *surrender!*

The crows hushed their stupid uproar; they had withdrawn into their fastness in the wood. Mr. Lindstrom and I stared deep into one another's eyes. Only three days ago Mr. Lindstrom had held me in his arms. How kind he had been! Yet there was a terrible intimacy in this moment: we were not teacher and student now but man and woman, face to face. Otherwise, the experience had little to recommend it.

He spoke at last.

"Get in the car. I'll drive you home. I'd like to have a little talk with your parents."

And so I rode the rest of the way home in Mr. Lindstrom's car. What irony that this event, which only minutes ago I would have believed the height of all possible happiness—even though it took place within the confines of an automobile—should in fact gain me nothing but wretchedness and misery!

I sat as far as possible away from him, clutching the door handle in readiness for our arrival. The horrors of the actual drive faded into insignificance; I barely realized my imprisonment. My soul was swamped, shipwrecked, sunken in a sea of hatred. Not that I hated him. Oh no! You would not believe that of me, would you?

No, it was his hatred for *me* in which I was drowning. I could not be mistaken; it was not dislike, or disapproval. It was hatred. The waters of the Antarctic could not have been colder or more unfriendly.

Mr. Lindstrom's car looked like him. I began to take notice of my surroundings. Details, so precious to a lover's heart, presented themselves to be catalogued, cherished. His car was charmingly, touchingly untidy. Litter from fast-food restaurants crunched underfoot, an old sweater huddled in the corner, books and dog-eared papers slid uneasily over the back seat. Yet even the beautiful homeliness of all this could not pluck my soul up from the briny depths.

When he finally pulled up in front of my house, I sensed that some of the rage had drained out of him. He craned his neck around and took a long thoughtful look at my home. I looked too and tried to see it through his eyes.

For one moment I did. I saw it as it must have seemed to him—the weedy, overgrown front yard, the shuttered windows, the creaking, decayed hulk of a building blotting out the pale stars now faintly glimmering in the east. A sense of loss swept over me. My home was a ruin, a disgrace, the haunt of owls and rats and mice, no haven fit for any respectable human family. I closed my eyes to escape the sight.

He spoke.

"Owl, I'm not coming in right now. I said I was going to talk to your parents, but I guess I'd better simmer down and think things over. Come talk to me after school tomorrow—can you?"

I nodded.

"Out you get, then. See you tomorrow."

I got out. "Thank you for the ride," I whispered.

"Oh, Owl, what nonsense." He smiled very faintly. "It was hardly a favor; you look half-dead of fright. Get in the house."

He idled the car, watching me. I pushed open the black wrought-iron gate, foolishly feeling like an actor thrust unprepared upon a stage. The hinges of the gate squealed and gibbered like a thousand souls in torment. Then it swung shut behind me with a melodramatic clang.

Under the hemlocks I walked, up the front steps, and through the heavy oak doors. The journey seemed to last years. I did not look back.

As soon as I stepped inside and knew myself to be hidden from his sight, I stopped. There seemed no point in putting one foot in front of another, no point in anything at all.

"Owl, darling! We've been quite nervous. Have you been hunting in the daylight?" My father popped his head out of the library.

"No."

"What is the matter, dearest? You're not still angry at your papa, are you?" He cocked his head on one side and shook a whimsical finger at me.

He sighed gustily at my lack of response. "I suppose I shall learn to love Mr. Lindstrom like a son in time." The lines of his face lengthened as I did not reply, and a note of self-pity colored his voice. "Owl, how can you be so cruel? I beg of you, don't look at me so sadly." He clasped his thin hands together and cracked his knuckles nervously.

I turned away impatiently. A beam of light from the streetlamp shone through the fanlight over the front doors and illuminated my face in the shadowed hall.

He gasped. "Owl, your face! You're ill! Your skin is— it's a terrible color."

"Oh, Owl, what a relief! Home at last. Did you have good hunting?" My mother bustled out from the kitchen, smelling of licorice and heal-all and so bursting with news that she paid no attention to my father's agitation. "By the way, such a funny thing, I've been waiting all afternoon to tell you. I was up in the attic, looking for one of those nice linen tablecloths to cut up for strainers, when I got to reading Emmy's diary—here, dear, take off your things and come into the kitchen—you know, Emmy Blackfield, your great-great-great-aunt on Daddy's side. Well—are you listening, dear? Because this is very interesting. She married a Lindstrom, isn't that marvelous? Do you think we could be related? Not very closely, of course, but how fascinating, don't you think?"

"Nesta," objected my father, momentarily forgetting his anxieties about my health in the heat of battle, "the man only moved here a few years ago; she said so. Our family, on the other hand, has lived in this town for two hundred years."

My father followed us into the kitchen, reciting in a high, fretful voice the names and addresses of all his ancestors. He sounded a little hoarse. Even through my cloud of misery, I could not help but suspect that the argument had been going on all day, my father anxious to reject relationship, my mother just as eager to claim it.

". . . And even if she had children, which I personally

doubt, there is no reason at all to suppose that this Lindstrom person is related to them in *any* way," he concluded triumphantly.

"Why not? It's an uncommon name."

"Nonsense. All of Scandinavia is crammed to the gills with them. Common as dirt."

"Oh, don't be such a silly. Let's see, Emmy's children would be your first cousins four times removed. Or would it be three times? I'm pretty sure they're not second cousins."

Wisely refusing to get caught up in this speculation (neither of my parents are strong on mathematics), my father changed his angle of attack.

"Nesta, you foolish woman, look at your daughter and stop babbling about my dead relatives. Look at her! She's dying! She's got jaundice or leprosy or something."

My mother turned and looked at me. In the gloom she could see neither my color nor my expression, but, alarmed, she lifted the lamp that flickered on the kitchen table and examined my face.

"Oh, Owl," she whispered. "What on earth is wrong?"

I could not tell them. I turned away and hurried up the stairs to my room without a word.

Usually a conscientious student, I did no homework that night. I flung myself out of the window into the gathering twilight to hunt with a ferocity I had never before

78

experienced. The little cakes I had eaten at Dawn's held me down no longer. I was nothing more than a consuming hunger, a gaping hole demanding to be filled.

The night was dry, the air bitterly cold. I killed again and again.

I did not visit Mr. Lindstrom's window that night.

Seven

"OWL, SIT DOWN." Mr. Lindstrom offered me a tired and worried smile. It was 2:30 in the afternoon of the next day. I had passed all the hours of that terrible day in numb expectation of this moment.

Was there ever a day so long? Entombed in my sorrow, I could not seem to feel anything. Teachers, puzzled by my poor preparation, twittered disapprovingly in the background. Even Dawn's friendly chatter had a disagreeable sound. I remembered her certainty that I would never mean anything to Mr. Lindstrom, and I could not forgive her.

In my heart there was nothing. Dust and ashes. A sense of waiting for the next blow to fall.

If you should happen to be a young person of spirit, my dejection may bring a curl of scorn to your lip. *What a milksop,* I hear you saying, *What a sack of soggy feathers.* Why didn't I show some self-respect? He was in the wrong, not I. He had misjudged me without proof.

You are absolutely right. I am ashamed. Love has brought me low indeed.

He smiled briefly at me during science period but did not speak.

"Owl," he said now, as we sat at the black-topped lab table in the deserted science room, "the facts are these. I was driving home from school when I saw a flock of crows attacking a girl. I immediately assumed the girl was guilty, even though I never saw her lift a finger to harm them. On consideration, I think I owe you an explanation."

He looked uncomfortable. "I was once, years ago, involved in a very ugly situation. It was . . . a child who tortured animals. Not a student of mine. A—a neighbor child." He shifted in his chair. A very shabby spiral notebook belonging to a careless student lay abandoned in front of him. His restless fingers began to pick at the curling cardboard.

"Oddly enough, crows were involved there too, but mostly the—the child hurt small things, helpless things."

Noticing my curious gaze he added, "This all took place far away from here. It was someone you don't know."

The image of Dawn as an overly dedicated biology student practicing her frog dissection skills on the next-door neighbor's Siamese cat had never once crossed my mind, I promise you.

"I became too—too emotional about that case. Even beyond my own personal involvement, the circumstances were especially painful to me. Biology, you know, is my field, and I'm fascinated by observing animals in the wild. Birds, especially. Birding is sort of a family tradition; all the Lindstroms have been bird crazy for generations. Sometimes I dream—" He stopped and coughed, then continued.

"So I suppose I'm a little more easily outraged than the average person. Anyway, I wasn't the ideal person to help that child. Even though . . ." He scowled at the long peel of cardboard he had just stripped from the notebook.

"Owl, please tell me." He looked up. "Did you hurt one of those crows? Throw a stone, anything? Please tell me the truth. It means a lot to me."

Thus entreated, I told him the truth. "I threw a stick at one of them."

"Ah! Why did you do that?"

"She pecked at my foot. The stick didn't hurt her."

He frowned. "'She'? How do you know it was a she?"

I hesitated. Mr. Lindstrom may have studied birds, but he could not know them as I did.

"It looked like a her," I said feebly.

He laughed. "Quite the naturalist." He looked at me steadily for a moment or so, trying to judge the truthfulness of my answers. "It's very unusual for a bird to attack a human like that. Maybe the crow was sick or starving."

A cynical "Hah!" nearly escaped me, remembering the glittering eyes, the glossy curve of that bird's breast. I managed to remain silent, however.

"But then the other birds—" Clearly Mr. Lindstrom was doing his best to believe my story, with considerable difficulty. His long slender fingers fiddled with the tattered notebook again. It was growing steadily more tattered with every passing moment.

"Tell me, has this ever happened to you before?"

Oh dear. He had begged me to be truthful, and I had given him my pledge, at least mentally.

"Yes."

He winced. "Often?"

"On occasion."

"Owl, you know, don't you, that Mrs. Walker in the guidance office is always ready to listen if you have problems, say, at home?"

This abrupt change of subject left me gaping.

"At home?" I inquired, mystified.

"Well, yes. Owl—" he took a deep breath—"you come from a—let's face it—an unusual family. A very old family in these parts, I understand, and one with strong, uh, traditions. Sometimes people in this position tend to feel cut off from the rest of society. They may get into, um, odd ways of thinking and acting. Do you know what I mean?"

"No."

"Oh. Maybe you'd like to talk to Mrs. Walker?"

"I'd rather talk to you," I said truthfully.

"That's very nice of you, but as I said earlier, I'm not very well equipped to deal with this sort of problem. In fact, I'm probably the worst person you could pick to talk to about it."

I mulled this over for a while. There was much here I did not understand. We both stared thoughtfully at the little pile of cardboard scraps that lay between us.

I shifted ground. "You think I hurt the crow."

"No! I don't know. I don't understand why crows would act like that." He stared moodily out of the window for a moment and then returned his attention to the notebook. The cover demolished, he had flipped it over to reveal a nearly undamaged surface. Gently his thumbnail teased up a corner of the top layer of cardboard. A ballpoint pen lying nearby served to punch a neat line of holes in the thin curl of cardboard.

To be perfectly frank, Mr. Lindstrom seemed to me to be making a lot of fuss over nothing. Random violence is exactly the sort of thing *I* associate with crows. It was sweet of him, though, to worry about that pack of worthless scavengers.

He turned and looked at me. His fingers ceased their irritable activity for a moment.

"Are you happy, Owl?"

What a question! Am I happy? How was I to sum up all the many conflicting emotions that I feel?

"Sometimes. Are you?"

He laughed shortly. "No! But that's not important. It was a stupid question, Owl. If you're happy sometimes, I guess you're doing okay." Briskly, he connected each hole with a large five-pointed star.

"If a problem comes up that talking will help, let me or Mrs. Walker know, will you?"

Before I could respond, a female student's head popped into the room. "Oh, 'scuse me, Mr. Lindstrom. I think I left my science notebook. I'm *really* sorry."

Suddenly aghast, Mr. Lindstrom's eyes focused on the sorry ruin in his hands. "Oh, er, Sandra . . ."

Tactfully, I rose to leave. Quickly thrusting the notebook into a drawer, he took advantage of Sandra's hunt for her ravaged possession to murmur, "And forget what I said just now."

At my questioning look, he reddened slightly and added, "About my own happiness. You—you caught me off guard."

Oh the *darling!* As if I could forget!

That boy *has* broken into Mr. Lindstrom's house. I knew it would happen as soon as I took my eyes off him. He has stolen a pup tent and assorted camping gear and set up camp a quarter mile into the woods behind Mr. Lindstrom's house.

How do I know the gear came from Mr. Lindstrom's house? The box in which he carried it into the woods was neatly labeled with Mr. Lindstrom's name and an Ohio address. Furthermore, it was marked "Camping Stuff" in his own dear handwriting. Obviously some time has passed since Mr. Lindstrom wrote it, for the ink has faded almost to invisibility, but my sharp eyes could not miss these tokens of him.

The miserable boy looked more miserable than ever. He hunched over a feeble flame, poking at it as though it were a personal enemy. In my human shape I would have felt rather chilly, crouched on a plastic ground cloth in the snow like that. Every once in a while he stood up and stamped his feet in the little clearing around his tent.

His wickedness is further demonstrated by his behavior toward me. He caught sight of me sitting in the pine tree over Mr. Lindstrom's tent.

"It's you!" he said, sounding surprised. Then his expression changed, like someone who has just realized that the faintly familiar face in the grocery store checkout line is familiar from news photos of a particularly loathsome escaped mass murderer. His brow darkened, making him look rather like a mass murderer himself.

His hand fumbled in the dirt by his fireside. He caught up a stone and threw it at me. Luckily, his aim was no better than his temper. The stone parted the branches to the left of me and fell harmlessly to the ground. To register my indifference to this maneuver, I did not move but continued where I sat, regarding him with deep disapproval. This seemed to enrage him still further. He leapt to his feet, grabbed up a large stick, and began to beat on the pine tree. Eventually I found the vibrations unpleasant and retreated to another tree a little further off but still overlooking him.

"Stupid *owl!* Sawdust for brains!"

Why he should choose to insult me personally, I could not tell you. I need hardly say that it was all very distasteful. I remained where I was, firstly because it seemed best to watch what he was up to and secondly because it irritated him so.

"Go away!" he cried, his voice high and thin. "Go away! Go kill something! Show us all how it's done."

I already had killed and was in no particular hurry to do so again. I noticed with some interest that there was no sign of food around his campsite. Perhaps it was hunger that made him so testy. Perhaps, but his eyes had a queer look to them. Frankly, he looked crazy.

He was so far gone in childish bad temper that he

actually came up and kicked the base of the tree where I now perched. Then he burst into loud sobs. His mouth hung open as he sobbed.

An unattractive youth.

At this point the owl family in the oak became aware of my presence in their territory and began to fuss. It would have been inexcusably rude to linger after they made their feelings clear, so I left, deeply disturbed. Why had the boy taken only camping equipment? I am no expert, but I believe that burglars generally take easily salable electronic equipment.

I decided that the boy was not a common thief. His parents, understandably anxious to be rid of him, had turned him out of the nest several years early. The theft of the camping equipment had provided him with some shelter against the wind and snow.

I almost felt sorry for the lad. Young ones whose parents turn against them have a bitter time of it in this hard world. His ugliness, after all, was not his fault. I myself was not precisely a beauty in human terms.

But something was clearly wrong with the boy's mind as well. Whether through unhappy circumstance or through a chemical imbalance in the brain, he had run mad. His parents, recognizing the uselessness of feeding or sheltering him any further, had pushed him out. It was sad, in a way.

Still, the fact that he had stolen from Mr. Lindstrom was enough to seal my dislike. Had the victim been anyone else I might have learned to pity the boy, but as it was, no arguments could move me.

A few minutes later I discovered Mr. Lindstrom still awake. His bed lay empty and disordered. This did not necessarily mean it had been already slept in; Mr. Lindstrom never makes his bed. This fact has always pleased me: I never make my bed either. We owls aren't fussy over these little details.

Mr. Lindstrom sat staring straight ahead into nothingness. He looked lonely, sitting in a cone of yellow light, pressed in by darkness on all sides. Could he be thinking of me?

The shiver of joy that ruffled my breast feathers was quickly stilled. His pose was not that of a lover. His face was difficult to read. There was much thoughtfulness, certainly, and concern. Yet where his thoughts led him, I could not guess.

He might be thinking of me, not as a lover but as a concerned teacher. At the moment that was enough for me. I was humbled by our recent coldness. I would be grateful for the slightest kindness on his part.

Then I realized that it was very likely the theft of the pup tent which left him so thoughtful and not any worry about me. Still, I had warmed myself over his imaginary concern, and that warmth did not entirely desert me as the night grew colder.

I have been watching that mad barn owl hunt. Never have I seen anything so pathetic in my life. He just launches himself off a branch like a suicide off a bridge. If you can believe it, he actually closes his eyes as he drops. He'll never last out the winter, poor demented creature.

The unfortunate screech owl family in the old oak has had a great deal to put up with from him. He seems determined to force some sort of relationship upon them while all that they ask is to be left alone.

Now, in the latter half of February, the little owl wife is probably in what is known as "an interesting condition." The first egg of the season may be expected at any time, or indeed may have already arrived. It is hardly a convenient time to entertain strangers. One would think that any owl, however poorly brought up, would have the simple tact to stay away at a time like that.

Yet that young male barn owl has been positively harassing the little family, popping up from nowhere and "who"-ing at them. He was at it again early this morning. After a laughable attempt to catch a meadow vole, he perched right next to the screech owl husband.

Naturally alarmed at being loomed over by so large a

cousin, the screech owl attacked. Evidently there were no eggs to protect as yet, for his strike did not connect. The little husband dared do no more than threaten.

The barn owl reacted as though assaulted by eagles. He nearly fell out of the tree, so great was his fright. He uttered the distress call of an immature nestling and flew away, swerving wildly to avoid a hemlock tree.

The screech owl now caught sight of me. Swelling dangerously, he glared blue murder at me. I quickly decided to make myself scarce. Despite the difference in our respective sizes, there was blood in his eye and he was defending his home.

On my way home a thought occurred to me. Could that barn owl have been brought up by a great horned owl instead of by his own parents? I have heard of such things. Cowbirds, I know, are such scandalously bad parents that they simply drop their eggs into any convenient nest and fly away, never giving them another thought. I shivered.

The great horned owl is respectfully known as "The Flying Tiger" by ornithologists and others familiar with their habits. I have never met a tiger, but I have made the acquaintance of a horned owl. I would far, far rather meet a tiger.

A barn owl raised by such terrible guardians would be unlikely to understand the niceties of barn owl behavior and might easily have learned their call: "H-h-hooo, hoo-o-o" instead of the rasping hiss normal to a barn owl. Strange, though, that he would be such a poor hunter. The ferocious appetite of a great horned demands excellent hunting skills to be satisfied.

Even more remarkable was that this miserable specimen could have shared a nest with two or three hungry great horned nestlings and survived.

• • •

It was difficult to be good. Lately, it seemed as though things were breaking up inside him, like a frozen lake in a spring thaw. He could almost hear the sound of water running under the big blocks of ice. He felt unstable, as though he might do or say anything.

Still, he tried. It had become a matter of overwhelming importance to him to get down to the cellar to look for the rats. He painted over the cracks in his peace as best he could by sitting and reading, motionless and expressionless, all day, every day.

They approved, or most of them did.

"Attaboy, Davey. You're back to bein' a good boy. Sure is a lot easier to handle when he's like this." They patted him on the back, congratulating him on his change in behavior. They even moved him back to his old room.

The doctor did not approve. "I thought we were making some progress with him at last," his doctor complained to the woman who sometimes came to see him. "But I'm afraid we're back to square one again." They thought he could not hear this because they were standing fifty feet away, down at the end of the long hallway from his room. All of them were amazingly stupid about things like that.

His old room was on a lower floor, closer to the cellar. The crazier you acted in this building, the nearer you rose to heaven. He had never been to that top floor. He would be afraid there; it was too high up. He imagined the sky beating upon the windows with padded, blind fists, demanding to come in, or demanding that he come out . . .

It was better to be here, with the basement so close, separated from him by only a few inches of flooring. He need only remain frozen for just a few more days, just until they forgot about him again. Then he would explore. Then he would find the rats.

Eight

THAT BOY IN THE WOOD fascinates me. Each night after I look in on Mr. Lindstrom I take a moment to observe the boy's camp. Though I know he is a wild, wicked creature, I cannot help but pity him. All his villainy will not save him from the wrath of these wintry winds.

There is some mystery about him. Perhaps it is this hint of romance, along with his pitiful condition, that touches my heart.

He does not eat. Once I found him in his usual position before the fire, holding an old dried-up apple in his hand. Tiny gnaw marks, brown with age, spiraled up one withered apple cheek. He must have fished it out of some animal's winter store of food. He watched the fruit as I might watch a mouse. Finally he brought it up to his nose and sniffed at it. He sighed and lowered it.

"No," he said, "I won't." His voice was low and hopeless, but nevertheless determined. He shut his eyes tightly and tossed the apple into the woods. His features grow daily sharper, the edges of his wide, flat cheekbones jutting through the skin.

Weight-loss diets are entirely foreign to owls. The great thing, we feel, is to stuff yourself as full as you can whenever you can. It's always wise to have something put aside for a rainy day. Damp weather means bad hunting for owls, and in a wet spring an owl can progress from stylishly slender to dead in a matter of days. We are not as plump as we look; our generous curves are almost entirely constructed of feathers.

Dawn, I know, feels that she ought to lose weight. Her excess poundage costs her prestige and mating opportunities. Personally, I cannot see that a wife who is apt to keel over in the first wet spell is much of an asset.

The boy is too thin already. This fasting is unnatural; he cannot keep it up much longer. I have toyed with the idea of leaving a few of my kills in the area. This odd impulse is difficult for me to explain.

Owls in general do not possess a social conscience. Every owl for her- or himself is our motto. When our children are small they are dear to us, but when they mature we recognize no further obligation to them. The greatest tie for us is the bond between a mated pair. Other owls are no more than competitors, rivals for the same warm and wriggling mouthful that ensures our daily existence.

I am, however, half human. It seems that my mixed heritage is tempting me to become some sort of a feathered do-gooder, a flying philanthropist. Have you ever heard of anything so odd?

I did once hear a tale about a holy man who was fed by ravens, but really, who could believe such nonsense? Ravens, of all birds! More likely they had been hoping to dine on *him* and dropped the food in a fright when they discovered he was still breathing. Ravens are closely related to crows. Enough said.

I believe this boy to be a victim of circumstances beyond his control. I have noticed a look of grim purpose in those dark haunted eyes of late. It would interest me very much to hear his story. I suspect that he is more sinned against than sinning.

Once or twice he has spoken to me.

"What are you looking at, hairball?" was his first utterance. Considered as a conversational opening, it was neither polite nor accurate, but his remark on the next occasion was more courteous.

"Why do you come and stare at me, bird?" His plain face looked years younger as he said it, and his huge bitter eyes grew sad. "You've come to sing my funeral dirge, maybe."

Sing! An owl! The boy's a perfect fool.

Yet the more desperate his circumstances grow, the more an air of dignity settles upon his scrawny shoulders, Yes, there is something about him, despite his surly ways.

"What about a love potion?" Dawn suggested, as we took turns peering into a microscope at a section of frog liver. "I mean, you've got a houseful of spells and stuff, don't you?"

I sighed. Dawn's efforts to assist me in my conquest of Mr. Lindstrom's heart were well meaning but a little wearisome. My mind was distracted in any case. Mr. Lindstrom was not here today. No, he wasn't sick, the substitute teacher said. They'd told her he was absent on family business. What family business could Mr. Lindstrom possibly have?

"I know your folks sell stuff like that. Why not try it? It'd even be free. Or maybe they'd get it for you wholesale, if they're cheap like my relatives."

I viewed the frog's liver in silence. I think it is a mistake to dissect your dinner. I have always been particularly fond of frog liver, but after drawing its cell structure, I don't know that I care for it anymore. It seemed such a waste, too, when there were so many empty bellies in the world.

Dawn joggled my elbow with ill-concealed impatience. "Well?"

I jumped, startled. I had been thinking of the boy in the forest. He might die soon if nothing was done. I found the thought distasteful. It would forever spoil that little wood for me. All the land about Mr. Lindstrom's house was sacred and ought to have no other emotional associations. I am too sensitive, I know, but there it is.

I considered Dawn's question. I did not exactly like to say anything critical about Mother's love potion. It was one of our best sellers. Most of our yearly school tax money came from love potions. Still, I did not place a great deal of reliance on its ability to win Mr. Lindstrom's life-long devotion.

"I can't ask my parents for a love potion," I said feebly.

Surprisingly, Dawn had no trouble believing this. "Yeah, I guess it would be pretty embarrassing, come to think of it. Well, all right. Why don't you just sneak some?"

"I beg your pardon?" I said icily.

"Oh, for crying out loud, Owl, it's not like you're stealing or anything. Not from your own parents."

"No?"

"Excuse me, Your Holiness. Of course, it's not worth it if you don't *really* want him." I could feel her eyes on my face, watching intently. I said nothing. She sighed deeply.

"You're just so passive about this whole thing. I mean, why don't you do something instead of just sitting around making cow eyes at him?" Dawn waved her arms energetically. Clearly, if Dawn were in my shoes, Mr. Lindstrom would be wooed, wedded, and bedded by now.

When I did not reply Dawn made a sort of hissing, exploding noise, which I took to express her mounting annoyance with me.

"Never mind," she said between clenched teeth. "Just because *you* won't do anything, that doesn't mean . . ." She glanced suddenly sideways at me and pressed her lips firmly together.

The bell rang.

"Bye." Dawn waved vaguely, her eyes thoughtful.

I *would* do something. I would save the boy from an icy grave and make Mr. Lindstrom admire me, both with the same stroke.

I would tell Mr. Lindstrom about the boy in the wood.

What a clever idea. I could not believe I had never thought of it before. Mr. Lindstrom has a soft spot for the weak and oppressed. Even those rascally crows moved him to compassion.

How dramatic it would be! But for me the boy would die of hunger and exposure. I would be a heroine in Mr. Lindstrom's eyes. In the weeks, nay, in the months to come, our joint rescue of the boy would form a bond, a subject of common interest and discussion.

And yet . . . what about the boy? What was he doing out there in the woods, anyway? Would he thank me for bringing his quest, or vigil, or whatever he was engaged upon, thus abruptly to an end?

Well, what else was I to do? Let him starve? Death was the only universal truth he was likely to discover in that grim little hollow. I owed the boy no special consideration. He had both assaulted and insulted me. If he did not appreciate my kindness, he was ungrateful as well as rude.

I would betray the boy to Mr. Lindstrom for the boy's own good. And mine too, of course.

This resolved upon, I decided to act quickly, before my sense of wrongdoing entirely overwhelmed my better judgment. Tonight would see the end of the boy's misery and the beginning of my joy. How could I bear to wait all the hours until I might start?

"Sk-k-k-kee!" I chattered in my excitement.

I planned first to make certain of the boy's presence in a suitably miserable state for rescuing. Then I would transform into human shape and approach Mr. Lindstrom on foot.

The blood sang in my head that night as I flew. If nothing else, I would speak with my love tonight, perhaps make him admire me a little. It would be something, to be abroad with him in the night, sharing my domain of darkness, solitude, and silence.

The boy was not there. I swore.

In my imagination I had led my love through the

wood, perhaps taking his hand as he stumbled on the crusted snow, reassuring him with a smile as some night noise startled his suburban sensitivities. Together we would coax the boy, the wild, injured thing, into accepting our protection and care.

This story must now be rewritten, and there were some advantages to the new version. If the boy had been at the camp, he would have been the star, not me. Great outpourings of warm blankets, food, and reassurance would be rushed to his aid. I would be all but forgotten.

I was at least in a position to restore Mr. Lindstrom's ravished household goods. After our walk through the dark and frozen wood, my darling might invite me into his home and serve me one of those gassy, bubbling beverages of which humans seem so fond. He might tell me how sorry he was to have misjudged me in the crow incident. As we sat in the warm yellow light of his living room, he might even be gently and tactfully led to speak of his secret sorrow.

This way, I wouldn't have to watch the boy being handed over to the county welfare workers.

Just as I prepared to fly away to Mr. Lindstrom's house, a dull thud to my right distracted me.

That foolish barn owl. He was up to his old tricks, trying to catch prey with his eyes shut. This time he had smacked his head smartly on a tree limb and was now flying dizzily about, three feet off the ground. His talons made a desperate grab at a branch as he passed over it. He overbalanced and ended up swinging upside-down in a very undignified position.

I must have made some sound. It was not a laugh, though it may have sounded that way. He looked up and saw me.

"WHO! WHO!" he bellowed, and flew straight at me. From an almost impossibly awkward position, he twisted upright and drove himself forward in one powerful, athletic movement.

Instantly he was upon me. Angry and frightened, I slashed at him with both beak and talon. He screamed. My beak only grazed his cheek feathers, but my claw held him fast. He suddenly ceased struggling and hung limp.

Stupidly I stood there clutching his heavy body, fighting for both physical and mental balance. Never had my owl nature and my human nature been more at odds. My human nature told me that I held in my talons a poor, pitiable fellow creature. My owl nature more urgently insisted that it was an enemy to be destroyed at once, before it regained its senses.

Strangle it quick and then dine at leisure, urged my owl mind.

No, no, murmured my human mind, distressed at this uncivilized thought.

Oh shut up and do it! ordered my owl mind in tones of authority older and more fundamental than the feeble protests of my human brain.

I very much fear that the argument would have been resolved in favor of a cannibal feast, but in the distraction of my mind, or minds, my grip loosened and he fell.

A crashing thump told me when he landed in the underbrush below. Almost immediately there were more crashings and a groan.

I was surprised. The groan was very un-owl-like. I flew down closer for a look. No owl was to be seen. Only that boy, naked as a newt, lying under the hemlock groaning. Those huge black eyes were closed in pain, or unconsciousness. One thin line scored his cheek. At the end of the scratch a drop of blood was forming. The blood glistened black against the gray, mud-colored skin. Three deep, savage slashes shredded his chest, and as I watched, the dark blood began to seep out, staining the snow a rich black.

Startled and not a little dismayed, I retreated to a higher branch to try to work out some reasonable explanation.

Perhaps the boy, having lost whatever wits he possessed, had taken to strolling through the forest in the nude. In this state of nature he had then been hit by the falling owl and was now blocking its relatively small body from my view. The owl might have clawed him in falling and in this dim light his red human blood would appear black.

I didn't believe a word of it. For one thing, my eyesight is too keen to be fooled in light far dimmer than this. For another, no footprints led up to the body where it lay in deep midwinter snow. And lastly, it had appeared to me that the boy was in the process of shepherding his wandering wits back into some sort of order, rather than the reverse.

As I considered this, I heard the rustle of a mouse below me. I pounced. In a trice I was back at my former station, the mouse dangling from my beak. Just as I was about to swallow the little tidbit, a thought occurred to me.

I flew to a very low branch just five feet above the boy's sprawled form. His eyes were open now. He put a hand to his chest and then examined the gore trickling down his fingers and wrist with an air of mild curiosity, as though the bloody hand belonged to someone else. He was in shock, a dangerous state for a person in his position. There was no sign of an owl.

He saw me, but his eyes were dulled and indifferent. I leaned over and gently released the mouse, aiming for the ground next to his right hand.

It never touched earth. His left hand flashed out and caught the mouse so swiftly that even my eyes could not follow the movement. He fumbled with the little corpse and then, holding it by the tail, dropped it into his mouth headfirst. He swallowed.

He closed his eyes momentarily. When he opened them, they were clearer. "Butterfingers," he said, with a weakly malicious smile at me.

Unfamiliar though I was with this term, I suspected it to be an uncomplimentary reflection on my act of mercy. I ignored this ingratitude. I had a great deal on my mind.

A very hungry human might easily eat a mouse. Yet even a human on the brink of starvation would not have been so prompt and enthusiastic. And even my dear parents, who have eaten their share of rodents, always insist upon boiling or broiling or baking perfectly good meat until it is all chewy and strange. Also, they never eat mice with the tail and skin intact and they always chew their dinner before swallowing.

To put off coming to a decision, and because the boy's eyes still burned with a famished light, I abandoned my reflections and put my mind to finding more food for the wretched creature. A vole was quickly captured and presented and even more swiftly eaten.

Automatically I returned to the pursuit of prey. After a shrew and two more mice had been dropped into the boy's begging hands, I found it difficult to stop the process of hunting and feeding. How satisfying it was, feeding the helpless thing! His attitude changed abruptly after the second meal. Once he got it into his thick head that the gifts of food were deliberate, his eyes followed me anxiously. Yet food was now the least of his needs. What good was a full belly to him if he died of exposure?

I puzzled over the problem. If the boy was a wereowl, why did he not transform? He would be far warmer in feathers than in bare human skin. His naked state was easily explained. He might not know the spells of binding which I used to spare myself that sort of embarrassment. My parents do have some useful knowledge.

To my relief the boy suddenly staggered to his feet clutching at his nakedness with thin arms. He blundered the twenty yards to his camp, hissing from the cold. He disappeared into the tent and then reappeared, clothed and bundled into a thick blanket.

Had he had time to tend to his wounds? They would fester without treatment. His clothing and blankets were filthy. I felt a flash of irritation. Having fed the boy, I was beginning to feel a stake in his survival. Did he want to die?

I noted with approval that he was painfully collecting twigs and branches for a fire. Satisfied that he could come to no harm for the moment, I flew away to hunt. Five small rodents are an insufficient dinner for an owl, let alone a growing human boy. My own stomach was beginning to demand food as well. This was going to be a busy night.

I flew on, searching for food.

• • •

Lying wakeful in his bed he knew it was time to go find the rats. The ward was quiet. Occasionally one of the others sighed or cried out; his were not the only bad dreams in this place. He got up and left, unseen, unnoticed. The man who was supposed to keep watch while they slept was himself asleep. Down corridors he went, down many stairs, moving as silently as a leaf blown across water.

The rats were there, sleek and secretive in the darkness of the cellar. He stared down at the rat in his arms, stroking the dead fur uneasily. He had caught the rat, but the sky had caught him. He growled softly. It was so unfair! How could he have known that the sky would find him in this low place, this big gloomy basement all damp and smelling of earth?

Someone had left the outside door to the basement open and the sky had gotten in. He stood in the narrow shaft of night air that spilled down the stairs and breathed its poisonous perfume.

A tear of self-pity trickled down his cheek. Why couldn't the sky leave him alone? Nothing would ever be the same again. His nutshell had cracked and could not be repaired. He almost smiled. The shell was broken and the nut was on the loose. He would be on his way in a few minutes. The forest was waiting for him, and the cold dark sky.

But first, he was hungry. He had not eaten for twenty-four hours. He hadn't wanted to be weighted down with their false food. Creeping downstairs in the dark he'd felt so light, as though he could have floated like a bubble.

Now he must eat. He clutched the rat to his chest and retired to a corner.

Nine

I FLEW ON, searching for food.

It seems I have done nothing else for days. I know now what it is to be a mother: unending toil and unending worry.

By daytime I am almost giddy from lack of sleep. My own hunger nags unceasingly. The hunting has been mercifully good, but the boy wants every bite. Still, I have acknowledged a hard lesson every parent must learn. If the chick is to eat, the parent must eat. I must keep up my strength or I will be too weak to feed Houle.

I named the boy Houle because it is the old Teutonic word from which the modern word "owl" is derived and because of the noise he makes when I do not feed him fast enough. Perhaps, too, I seek to bind him to me by giving him a name that rhymes with my own. I have no further proof that he is an owl; he has not transformed once in the three days in which I have been feeding him.

I have tested him by dropping various food items that a human might like but which would not interest a bird of prey: potatoes from our root cellar, a hard candy dropped on the school grounds, one of my mother's loaves of fresh bread. He treats these offerings with a sort of baffled contempt.

"Rabbit fodder!" he mutters before tossing them into the bushes, or, in the case of the loaf of bread, bunting it like a football into the crotch of a nearby tree. I ought to feel annoyed by his bad manners, but what I chiefly feel is pride in his newfound strength.

I think he is a wereowl.

I have not seen his wounds since the night they were inflicted. I can tell, however, that they still pain him. The grip of a barn owl is nothing to laugh at, even for a human. If it was I who administered the slashes on his chest, I did so to another and smaller owl, whom I could easily have killed. No wonder he caught his breath with pain as he lofted my mother's bread into the tree.

Something has happened that causes me great concern. Mr. Lindstrom still reigns supreme in my heart, of course, but I simply am unable to think of him or visit him very often these days.

Last night, flying wearily back to camp, I found myself over his back yard. I am afraid the only reason I stopped was because I feared that without rest I would tumble right out of the air. Someone was standing, motionless, in the back yard. It was not Mr. Lindstrom. It was no one I had ever seen before.

She was barefoot in the snow, her hair hanging down around her shoulders, uncombed and unkempt. She wore a long white robe and she was weeping bitterly.

"Please," she whispered, almost too low for even my hearing to detect, "Be safe. Oh, please be safe."

She sobbed. The wind picked up the small sound and blew it away into the darkened woods.

"I'm s-sorry," she pleaded, her voice thick and distorted with grief. Then she bowed her head and was silent.

Decidedly disturbed by this apparition, I checked Mr. Lindstrom's bed. He was not in it. One lamp was on in the living room, but I could not detect Mr. Lindstrom's form by its light. Was he sitting somewhere in the dark, watching the madwoman in the snow? The situation was positively creepy.

I wondered suddenly if what I had seen was a ghost. A woman in white, weeping in the snow: that sounded about right, but she belonged in the grounds of a house like mine, not in the back yard of Mr. Lindstrom's ten-year-old split level.

I could find Mr. Lindstrom nowhere. Where was he, at one o'clock in the morning on a school night? He ought to be in bed. These late hours would be the ruination of his health. Uneasily I shifted from claw to claw on my perch. I really ought to be getting back to Houle. He would be hungry again.

A cry sounded off in the wood. It was not Houle, but I started guiltily. *I can't be two places at once,* I grumbled, feeling harassed. Mr. Lindstrom was a grown man and probably perfectly capable of handling a disembodied spirit without my aid. Houle needed me. At last I flew away, very troubled in my mind.

"You look awful," Dawn remarked critically.

I supposed I did look awful. I certainly felt awful.

"Like you haven't slept in a week."

It seemed twice as long. It was lunch hour of the next day. I sat with my head propped in my hands, trying to sneak a quick nap while Dawn munched and slurped her meal opposite me.

"I haven't slept so hot lately, either," she confided. "The cops are looking for an escaped convict near my neighborhood, I hear."

I opened my eyes.

"Yeah, a young one, I think. I don't know where he came from. We haven't got any prisons or reform schools around here that I know about. My mom thinks maybe he's got relatives in the area."

I thought of the policemen searching the forest for him and my nails dug into the wooden seat of my chair.

"Wow! Hey, Owl, you know your eyes just went all

red? It was weird! Like some kind of—what're you doing to that chair? Jeez, Owl, you've got big hunks of wood under your nails."

I quickly blinked and forced myself to relax.

How was I to keep Houle safe? The problem nagged unmercifully at my exhausted mind all day. Instead of drowsing peacefully through my classes, I sat tensely upright, brushing aside the scholastic inquiries of my teachers. They seemed rather displeased, but I had no time to spare either for their feelings or for the voyages of Magellan. My Houle might be taken at that very moment.

The easiest solution would be to bring him to my own house. Unfortunately, four long miles lay between Houle and my home on Muldaur Street, and he was still not very strong. Communication could be a problem, too. He knew me only as an owl. I would have to approach him in my human shape, and he would run away before I could so much as speak to him.

After some hesitation I decided to transform in front of him. This ran counter to all my deepest training and instincts, but it seemed the only way. I must decide to trust him, that was all.

I flew straight to Houle's camp after school. He must be moved immediately. He was too close to Mr. Lindstrom's neighborhood for safety. Mr. Lindstrom himself might put two and two together and deduce something from the theft of his camping gear. He might have already done so.

It gave me a queer feeling to think of Mr. Lindstrom as Houle's enemy and therefore mine in this matter. I had meant him to be Houle's salvation, but the time for that had passed. I could no more have betrayed Houle than I could have betrayed Mr. Lindstrom himself.

Once again Houle was not there, just when I had most counted on his presence. I hissed with irritation. Really, the boy was too annoying. Or—a pang of fear shot through me—had he already been taken?

No, I did not think so. The camp was undisturbed. The forces of law and order would have torn the place apart during his capture. I knew without question that he would resist to the utmost of his ability.

My heart rose at the sudden thought that, frightened by his searchers, he might have transformed at last. I scanned the surrounding terrain, hunting for the mad barn owl. Strange to think that I would have given one of my very eyes for a sight of that pitiful excuse for a bird.

He had always hunted, if you could call it hunting, the area around the camp. I searched in ever-widening circles, my heart despairing. He, who could barely fly straight, would never have flown so far away unless he was really frightened.

I will find you, Houle, I thought grimly, however long it takes.

It took five hours. The boy lay flat on his back in the snow under a little crab apple tree in a back yard just down the street from Mr. Lindstrom's house. He was staring up at the sky and reciting poetry.

"'The Owl and the Pussycat went to sea,'" he muttered. "Yeah." He recited:

"'The Owl and the Pussycat went to sea
In a beautiful pea-green boat,
They took some honey, and plenty of money,
Wrapped up in a five-pound note.
The Owl looked up to the stars above
And sang to a small guitar.'"

He mumbled a bit and then began shouting weakly. I glanced nervously around.

"'And there in a wood a Piggy-wig stood
With a ring at the end of his nose!'"

"Ssshh!" I warned. Although it was only an owl's hiss, he heard and obeyed. His voice dropped to a murmur for several lines but slowly gained in volume as he neared the end of the poem.

"'And hand in hand, on the edge of the sand, They danced by the light of the moon,'" he announced loudly.

"Sssshhh!"

"Oh all right," he said peevishly. "I'm done."

After a brief pause, he added, "By Ogden Nash."

"Edward Lear," I corrected, though of course he could not understand me.

"Lear, I mean," he said, and glared at me with mad, fever-bright eyes. "Lear. I knew that. Hey, Owl, you elegant fowl, looky this. 'Nature, red in tooth and claw.'" He waved his hand at me.

The color red is the first to fade in dim light, but streetlights and house lights illuminated the neighborhood even for human eyes. Houle's hand was sticky with bright red blood. If it belonged to him it certainly knocked out any idea of his being a wereowl.

"Wanna see something pretty, Owl? Pretty pictures. Pretty." He waved his gory hand again. "You're a good listener, Owl, know that?" he continued, as I turned to look in the direction he had indicated. "I'm not much of a talker, usually. I'm hot," he complained suddenly. "Hot. It's too hot in here." He scrubbed a handful of snow across his face.

The drawings were fifty feet away, on the back porch.

Houle had drawn crude symbols in a wavering line all along the white-painted porch railings. Most of them seemed to be animals although it was difficult to be sure. The blood used as a painting medium had dripped and run, and bloody fingerprints smeared the outlines.

Houle's footprints were clearly visible in the snow. I knew that I had to get him to shelter immediately, but his tracks led me unwillingly on, to the next house nearer Mr. Lindstrom's. Yes, there were drawings here, too, more than at the last house.

Swiftly I flew to the next house. As I retraced Houle's route, I saw that each decorated area was bigger than the last. Which meant that Mr. Lindstrom's, the house nearest the wood from whence Houle had come . . .

Staring at the mess on Mr. Lindstrom's house, I groaned aloud. Here was madness, here was evil.

I knew that the boy was ill, that festering wounds sometimes bring fever. When hurt creatures behave strangely, it means only that their brain is disordered from disease. He would either die of it or he would not. Most likely he would.

Yet I was horrified beyond all reason. Where had all this hatred come from? It zigzagged up and down the siding of Mr. Lindstrom's house, out of control, a firestorm of rage, a torrent of malice and abuse.

These crude animal forms ought to have seemed harmless, the scribblings of a child, but they did not. There was a malignant purpose behind them; a spell that worked for evil, an incantation that cursed my darling's house.

Why, Houle? I begged, *Why this house?* It could so easily have been another, and then how much easier it would have been to understand and pity you.

I must move him immediately. Every moment I delayed brought him closer to his death. Yet how hard it was to feel compelled to press this deadly little serpent to my bosom. I sighed and flew slowly back to him.

He needed blankets and medicine and, if possible, central heating. My home was too far away. He could never walk that far in his condition.

I must turn him in to the police, just to save his life.

"Owl," murmured Houle, "don't leave me. Don' go." He stirred, and his glittering eyes focused on me. "Keep 'em away from me. Owl?"

I groaned. Of all the corny, clichéd situations. A deathbed request! Why, even Dawn, with her romantic nature, wouldn't . . .

Dawn! This was Dawn's neighborhood, too. Only a hundred yards away or so stood Dawn's overheated, overfurnished house, a house undoubtedly bursting at the seams with clean sheets and down comforters and thermometers.

But could Dawn be trusted? I did not know. I simply did not know. I had no experience of the daily give-and-take of human life, of petty betrayals and small loyalties. How does one detect malice behind a smooth, smiling, pink face? Humans seem to navigate the shifting winds of their own complicated personalities with some success, but I knew that this skill required many years to learn. How on earth was I to judge?

Still, even if she proved a bent reed, I would be no worse off than before. If she told her mother, Mrs. Mitchell would at least summon the medical attention he needed.

But I hoped Dawn could be trusted. Houle had been healing in the woods until this unfortunate setback. His mind had been growing stronger and more wholesome every day.

If he had indeed escaped from a reform school, the social workers and psychologists had already had their chance at him. They had not healed him. The wilderness was his medicine, and it was up to me to see that he survived the dose.

I felt certain that Houle would rather die than go back. If I was wrong . . . well then, I was doing a dreadful thing. There could be no forgiveness for the risk I was about to take with his life.

• • •

"Hello, is Dawn there, please?"

Mrs. Mitchell's eyes grew almost as big as, well, mine. She caught my elbow and drew me into the house as though afraid I might run away.

"How did you get here?" she demanded. "Dawn says your family doesn't have a car."

"I fl— I walked."

"All that way? In the dark?"

I nodded.

"Don't you know there's an escaped convict running loose? Goodness, child, I can't think why your mother let you come."

I tried to imagine my mother forbidding it. She knew my life had more than its share of risks. She worried but she accepted it because she must.

"Dawn!" Mrs. Mitchell shouted. "Come here. You've got company."

In the living room a plump, balding man was watching television. There was no sign of Dawn's hated younger brother.

"Ken," Mrs. Mitchell said, pushing me forward, "this is the Tycho girl. Remember? I told you she came home one day with Dawn."

"'Lo," said Mr. Mitchell, without lifting his eyes from the television set. "How ya doing?"

"Very well, thank you," I replied politely, if untruthfully. My mind was busy. Where would we put Houle? It was hard to believe that Houle and Mrs. Mitchell could coexist in this small house without disaster.

"Owl! What're you doing here?" Dawn had appeared with a romance novel tucked under her armpit.

"Really, Dawn!" Forgetting her own abrupt inquiry at first sight of me, Mrs. Mitchell rebuked her daughter. "Manners!"

"I wondered if you'd care to go for a walk."

Mrs. Mitchell shrieked.

"A *walk*?" Dawn stared as if I had proposed shooting her from a cannon.

Even Mr. Mitchell looked up from his television program. "Dawn? A walk? That's a laugh." He did not laugh, however.

"No, Dawn, absolutely not. Why don't you take Owl up to your room? I'm sorry, Owl, but I just don't think it's safe. I'll drive you home when I pick up Dawn's brother from soccer practice."

This whole thing was a mistake; I could see that now. How could I have chosen so wrongly? Houle was dying. At this very moment his life was seeping out into the snow.

Dawn must have seen something in my face. She came forward quickly and murmured in my ear, "Hang on. We'll go, don't worry." More loudly she said, "Yeah, let's go up-stairs, Owl. Nobody's gonna snoop around and listen. Right, Mom?"

"Dawn!"

"Right, Mom?"

"I wouldn't dream of it. You girls can talk secrets till the cows come home. *I'm* going to call your Aunt Gina," and she flounced out of the room. We heard a door slam in another part of the house.

"So that's okay," Dawn said. "My dad never notices anything, and El Stinko isn't here, so we're in the clear." Instead of going upstairs as advertised, she walked boldly over to the hall closet and donned her coat and scarf. "Watch this," she whispered with a grin.

"I'm going out for a walk with Owl, Dad. That okay with you?"

"What? Oh sure," responded Mr. Mitchell, deep in his crime show. "Havagootime."

Ten

Extracting Dawn from her house was really the least of my troubles, but it raised my spirits somewhat. I had forgotten what a good manager Dawn was.

"Wait," I said. "Have you got a blanket?"

"A—? Well, I guess we could get the one from the car without making too much racket."

She did not ask what it was for. She appeared to be enjoying herself.

To my surprise, the garage was heated. How astonishingly tenderhearted they were! They did not even like their automobiles to become chilled. How could I not trust such kind people? Would they turn a shivering, helpless boy over to the police?

Well, yes, I thought, Mrs. Mitchell would. She would be terrified of Houle and all he represented. She would be even more frightened when she saw Mr. Lindstrom's house. Certainly she would never believe that it would be a kindness to keep Houle hidden rather than delivering him to a hospital bed. I might even have my hands full convincing Dawn of that.

I could only hope Dawn would not see the bloodstained pictures. There was no real reason why she should. The closest ones were not very near, and it was nighttime.

"Where to, O Queen? Your wish is my command." She stood by the door to the garage, her arms folded around a fat red plaid car blanket.

"This way."

He had not moved except to close his eyes. He seemed to be sound asleep. I felt faintly troubled by his air of peaceful repose. Surely he could not be comfortable, asleep in the snow. Yet his thin mouth curved gently in a blissful smile, and his expression was almost that of a sweet-tempered child. His troubles lifted, he had hoisted his sails and was flying away into a great empty sky.

Dawn drew in her breath. "It's the convict, huh? Boy, is he ugly or what?" She hunched her shoulders up suddenly and clutched her arms protectively. "Brrr. Looks like he could slit your throat with one hand tied behind his back. With both hands tied behind his back," she added after studying him further. "He'd use his teeth."

Annoyed at this unkind description, I was about to offer a spirited reply, but I recognized that this would merely waste time.

"He's dying," I contented myself with saying.

"Yeah, it's not too good that he's asleep like that. I

think that's what happens when you freeze to death. You just feel all cozy and warm and fall asleep." She seemed to remember the blanket in her arms because she shook out the folds and laid it cautiously on his slumbering form.

"You wanna stay with him while I go call the cops?" Dawn asked.

I was silent for a moment, considering how to present my plea.

Dawn went on, misinterpreting my hesitation. "Sorry, stupid question. I know *I* wouldn't want to be left alone with him. He's not going anywhere. Unless he's just faking it, waiting for a chance to pounce. Hey, what's that junk all over his hands?" She bent closer, peering with her weak human eyes.

"Owl . . . Owl?" she whispered in some agitation. "He's got blood on his hands."

"I believe it's his own blood," I replied, although I was not entirely certain that this was so.

"Oh. Gross. Well, come on, let's get outta here. This guy gives me the cold horrors."

"No, Dawn, please," I said humbly. I did not know what else to do. "Please." I turned to look at him lying there.

Dawn stared at me. "You—you can't mean what I think you mean. No!" she said when I simply looked at her. "No, Owl, forget it. You're crazy! You're out of your mind. Look at him. He's like a mad dog or something.

You'd probably be poisoned if he even breathed on you." She stared at me some more. "Give me a *break,* Owl," she said, her voice rising. I hushed her.

"Give me a break, Owl," she whispered fiercely at me. "This is real life. Even if I wanted to help you save this psycho, he's in big trouble. He might have frostbite. He looks sick to me," she added accusingly.

"He is," I said somberly. "Very sick."

"Well there. You see? And he's bleeding."

"I don't think so, not anymore. It's dried blood."

"So big deal. If the cops get him they'll at least take care of him."

"If he's not well in a day or two, we could call them."

"And where would we keep him?" she demanded.

"Well . . ."

Dawn's jaw dropped until I thought it would unhinge itself.

"You expect me to hide this deranged criminal in my house? Exactly where? In my bedroom closet? In a shoe box, maybe?"

Disregarding this last suggestion, which could hardly have been serious, I considered. A closet? Well, not ideal, perhaps, but . . .

"Owl Tycho, get that look off your face. Owl, stop it! I won't, I tell you. This is the stupidest thing I've ever heard. Do you hear me, Owl, *I will not do it.*"

• • •

In the end it was the garage we chose. It would simply have been too difficult to smuggle Houle inside the house and up the stairs. Even if Mrs. Mitchell had still been talking to her sister and Mr. Mitchell was still engrossed in his television show ("No question about that," Dawn volunteered), it was simply too risky. The most devoted fan of TV drama could not help but notice his daughter and teenage friend wrestling the unconscious, blood-spattered form of a sinister-looking young man up the stairs to her bedroom.

Then, too, Dawn's refusals lost their intensity when she realized that she would not have to sleep in the same room with my poor Houle.

"We always lock the door to the garage anyway," she mused. "Maybe I could push some furniture up against it, too. But I *won't* feed that thing. I won't, you hear me?"

"Some water will be sufficient," I replied. I doubted that Dawn would wish to donate her hamster to the cause, and Houle did not seem to relish any other sort of food.

"No! I won't go near it. It gives me the creeps. Why are we doing this, anyway? Never mind," she said suddenly, with a sharp look at me. "I can guess, I s'pose."

I was surprised, frankly. I knew that Dawn was very quick and clever in her observations, but that she should guess at my motives when I hardly understood them myself

127

was really remarkable. I was almost tempted to ask her why we *were* doing it, purely for my own information.

She surprised me still more when she added quietly, "I guess I could give it—I mean him—some water. And some food."

"That is very kind," I said, "But I can feed him. I don't think he'll eat now. I'll be back in the morning and bring some medications from my parents."

Dawn's eyes brightened. "We've got lots of old medicines in the bathroom. I'll bet there's something we could use."

Thinking of Dawn's drawers full of cosmetics, and the results she had obtained with them, I declined as politely as I could.

He was a dead weight at first. Dawn and I had great difficulty lifting him. His jacket slid up his back as we trundled him along so that his bare skin scraped across the snow. I winced at the thought of how we must be hurting him, but he did not stir until we paused, panting harshly, outside Dawn's garage.

We laid him down to rest our aching arms for a moment before the last haul into the garage itself. Puffs of frosty breath materialized briefly over our heads and vanished again in a ragged rhythm.

Houle opened his eyes. Dawn made a queer gulping noise, like someone who has just swallowed a golf ball.

He did not move at first, his big, black eyes searching our unfamiliar faces. I could see the calculation behind them, and the terror. I had to hope that his illness had weakened him enough that he would not be a danger to us.

He lurched halfway to his feet and then overbalanced and fell. He lay there with one hand up, warding us off, teeth bared. He made a hissing, growling noise terrible to hear.

I glanced at Dawn to see how she was taking this. She was very white in the moonlight, and her eyes were big as saucers, but she was holding her ground. "Do something, Owl," she said.

I turned back to Houle.

"Houle," I whispered, "Houle! It's all right. Hush now, Houle."

I had forgotten that he did not know his name—how could he? He seemed puzzled. He hushed and looked at me with fever-glazed eyes.

"Owl?" he muttered. "Owl? Where? Wherza owl?"

Inspired, I nodded urgently. "Yes, Owl! Owl wants you to go with us. Owl told us to take care of you."

"Huh?" said Dawn.

"Shush."

Houle considered this for a moment. A neighboring dog, who had ignored our muffled din up until now, began to bark. Houle flinched, and the mad, panicky look came back into his eyes.

"Houle, Houle," I crooned, alarmed. "Remember, Owl wants you to come with us." The dog stopped barking.

His eyes cleared. "Yes," he said. "All right, I'll come."

The sanity of this reply seemed to reassure Dawn somewhat. I bent to help him and, hesitating, she followed. He managed only a few staggering steps before he once again lost consciousness. We stifled our grunts as he slumped against us, his head lolling forward. We were inside now, at least.

"Where?" I breathed.

"Here," Dawn puffed. She tugged us toward the back of the garage. It was a large garage, and an area about eight feet by ten had been converted into a workshop. It had been partitioned off from the rest of the space and contained a workbench, a jumble of tools, some cardboard boxes, several broken chairs, and a large dog bed.

"Sorry," Dawn hissed through her teeth. "Best I can do."

"Where's the dog?" I asked, as we lowered Houle onto the bed. Houle did not strike me as a dog lover.

"Dead." Dawn and I stood breathing heavily over Houle's inert body. "Two years ago. Mom says I should just get another one, but I can't." She sniffed a little, whether from the cold or with emotion over the dearly departed I could not tell.

"I'm sorry."

Dawn nodded. "Snowball was one of the best," she said mournfully.

"We need more blankets," I said. It was warm in the garage, but not as warm as in the house.

"And a coupla pillows," Dawn volunteered, business-like again after her moment of sentiment. "He's bigger'n Snowball."

"And a thermometer," I offered.

"And aspirin," Dawn said. "We can give him aspirin, can't we? Oh, come *on*, Owl. It'll bring down his fever."

This seemed reasonable.

"What's the matter with him, Owl? It's not just the cold, is it?"

I shook my head. Kneeling in front of him, I unzipped his jacket and gently peeled up his dirty, stained shirt. I could tell by the small gasp from Dawn that she saw them too: four discolored, raised ridges, each about five inches long. Oh yes, they were infected all right. But I saw no source of fresh blood. That meant the blood on his hands was not his own. I hoped Dawn would not notice.

"What happened to him?" she whispered in awe.

I shook my head. I didn't know, not for sure, anyway.

"Looks like he had a disagreement with the devil, doesn't it? What else has claws like that? That is absolutely gruesome."

I laid a cool palm on his skin and he shivered in his sleep. How hot was he? 104 degrees? 105 degrees? Much too hot. I covered him back up.

"We'll need hot water, Dawn." I was remembering my mother's warm poultices and teas.

"Yeah, no problem. We've got a hot plate. I can just leave a kettle of water out here, and you can heat it up when you need it."

I stood up and we left him.

Eleven

As we walked in through the door to the house, Mrs. Mitchell materialized in front of us.

"And where have you two been?" She looked a trifle testy. Her hands were on her hips and her elbows stuck out at a militant angle.

"In the garage."

"What were you doing out there?" she asked suspiciously.

"A science project," Dawn lied coolly.

"Oh," said Mrs. Mitchell, evidently knocked off her perch by this reply. "Your father didn't know where you were, and I couldn't find you anywhere. I didn't realize you had a project due."

"Neither did I," Dawn answered, this time with a nearer approach to the truth. "Owl only just remembered it herself." Dawn began to elaborate on this fairy tale. "She walked all the way over here to tell me about it. See, Mr. Lindstrom sent me out of the room with a message to um . . . the school nurse, and he assigned it while I was gone. Mr. Lindstrom told Owl to tell me, only she forgot.

And then she couldn't call me 'cause they don't have a phone. I think it was *very* nice of Owl," she concluded severely.

I held my breath to hear Mrs. Mitchell's response to this rigmarole. Mr. Lindstrom had been absent for several days, but perhaps she didn't know this.

"Why, Owl, that *was* very nice. Well, what is this science project?"

If I thought that this would stump Dawn I couldn't have been more wrong.

"Small mammal anatomy," she replied crisply. "It's a long-term project—but"—Dawn looked at me—"I hope it's not *too* long-term. Owl and I are gonna catch a field mouse, skin it, and identify its internal organs. We're gonna kinda stake it out on a board and label it. We better get some formaldehyde from Mr. Lindstrom, don't you think, Owl?"

I nodded.

"Oh, how disgusting!" Mrs. Mitchell showed no enthusiasm for this scientific inquiry. "Where did you get such a horrible idea?"

"Mother, please! It was Owl's idea." This, of course, was entirely false. I cannot imagine myself suggesting such a plan. What a waste of a mouse!

"Oh! I beg your pardon, Owl. It's just . . . that sort of thing makes me a little ill."

"That's why we're doing it in the garage. Dad won't be working out there this time of year, and you won't be bothered by the sight of it or"—she paused significantly—"by the smell."

Mrs. Mitchell gave a little shriek.

"Oh, but Dawn, I have to go out to that garage every day to get the car. I might see the . . . thing."

"I'll tell you what we'll do," Dawn offered generously. "We'll hang an old sheet across the doorway so you won't be bothered."

"Oh, all right."

"And," Dawn added, "you can get Dad to back your car out so you don't have to go into the garage at all."

"Yes, that's a good idea. Formaldehyde gives me such a headache. I remember from school. Well, all right. Have you two finished talking about it? Because it's time to go pick up your brother, and I wanted to drive Owl home at the same time."

"Sure. Don't worry, Owl, I'll take care of that stuff we talked about."

When Mrs. Mitchell turned away, Dawn said, "That's okay, then. Mom's the only one we have to worry about. I could be dissecting a hippopotamus out there and Dad'd never notice. My brother's a total dim-bulb, and he's never here, anyway. We should be safe for a day or two. Better tell your buddy to be quiet."

"He'll be quiet," I promised.

"Mmm. He'd better. I gotta tell you, Owl, this is a crazy thing we're doing. It's just as well we're both underage. I've got a really bad feeling that this is illegal. Only thing is, I don't think he's really a convict—more like a loony."

I nodded slowly. I too had sensed the madness in Houle's eyes from the first moment I met him.

It suddenly struck me that perhaps I ought to thank Dawn for all her efforts.

"This is extremely kind of you," I began awkwardly. "I cannot tell you how much I appreciate—"

"Oh, that's okay. It makes a change, anyhow." She grinned. "Maybe this is what you had in mind when you said I ought to take up a life of crime, huh?"

"I never—"

"Just kidding, Owl."

"I'll be back very early tomorrow morning to feed him," I told her. "You needn't get up. Can you make sure the side door to the garage is unlocked?"

"Hey, I can feed him. We've got lots of food."

This was a puzzle. I could not reveal Houle's diet, and the excuse that her mother might notice the missing food was obviously nonsense. Dawn could easily devour twice the daily ration for a sickly Houle without causing any comment in this household.

I just shook my head.

"But, Owl, it's *four miles* to your house."

"He is my responsibility," I said with dignity. "You have done more than enough already."

The honk of an automobile horn sounded in the driveway.

"That's my mom," Dawn said. "You better go now."

I hesitated.

"It was clever of you," I suggested, "to think of that science project idea so quickly. What made you think of dissecting a mouse?"

"It *was* clever, wasn't it? Oh, just because I figured you could supply the mouse without any trouble."

With the deepest of misgivings, I asked, "And why was that?"

"Because," she answered rather coldly, "I saw the way you looked at my Brownie."

"Your—?"

"The hamster, Owl, the hamster."

My mood of hope and cautious confidence considerably dampened by this parting shot, I climbed into Mrs. Mitchell's automobile.

I did not insist upon "walking" home. I could tell by the way the Mitchells referred to my supposed four-mile hike that this was considered an athletic exertion quite out of the common way. At any rate, I had become so accustomed to riding in cars and buses lately that I almost forgot to feel frightened. My mind was so crammed with such a number of hopes, fears, and morbid imaginings that I had no room for any other sensations.

Mrs. Mitchell prattled on about Dawn's social adjustment, and science projects, and the extreme delicacy of Mrs. Mitchell's nervous system.

"I can't even cut up a chicken," she was saying. "That's why I don't cook much. That awful, puckered pink skin! Eeugh!" She shuddered. "Not like that weirdo in the woods, I guess."

My ears pricked up immediately.

"You really ought to be more careful. It was very nice of you to walk over here to tell Dawn about that project, but you could just as well have told her tomorrow. I hear he's a real sicko, that guy. I hope they catch him."

"Is he—is he wanted for committing a crime of some kind?" I faltered.

"I don't think so. Apparently he did some awful stuff as a little kid—they didn't say what exactly. The reporter on Channel Two dropped some heavy hints about Satanism, but that's silly; the guy was hardly more than a baby when they shut him up in the nuthouse. He's been there ever since."

"I see," I said sadly. My poor Houle. So this was his story.

"Well, don't take it so personally, Owl," Mrs. Mitchell said jovially. "Sensitive type, aren't you?

"Okay, now. Is this the right place?" She pulled up in front of my house. "Dumb question, huh? Like I don't know the Tycho house. Don't your folks even leave a porch light on for you, for heaven's sake?"

"A light on the porch?" I repeated, surprised. "The wind would blow it out."

"Good grief! You mean Dawn wasn't kidding when she said you don't have electricity? That's absolutely incredible!" She peered around the dark yard and scanned the shabby facade of the house, dimly lit by the nearby streetlamp. "Could stand a little maintenance, couldn't it?" she said critically. "Still, I guess that's part of the charm, such as it is. Well, out you get. See you soon, anyway, if you and Dawn are working together on that *gruesome* project."

Strangely enough, Mrs. Mitchell's frank comments about my home did not disturb me nearly as much as Mr. Lindstrom's carefully expressionless face as he looked at the house.

Mr. Lindstrom! When had I last thought of him? I hadn't seen him in days. Why, he could be dead for all I knew. My heart smote me with an almost physical pain. How could I be so faithless, so inconstant in my love?

How dreadful! How humiliating. I had fallen even below the human standard of love. I could not fall much lower.

"Owl? Have you gone into a trance or something? I've said good night three times."

"I beg your pardon. Good night, and thank you for bringing me home."

"Look, I'm sorry if I seemed a bit critical of your house. I'm like that—tactless. Dawn is too, though she's sharp enough about people."

"No, no, not at all," I murmured meaninglessly, and stumbled away, up the steps to my home.

"Mother, what would you advise for a man—a young man about my age—with infected chest wounds and a high fever?"

"An immediate visit to Doctor Grimsby," my mother responded promptly. "Or the emergency ward of the hospital, I suppose, if he were really bad."

"No, no," I said crossly, "an herbal remedy. Surely you know something that would help him."

"Oh yes, but darling, you really shouldn't fool around with serious illnesses like that. It's true that a slice of moldy bread held up to a wound may provide enough penicillin to fight an infection, but then again it may not. It is simply too risky, I'm afraid."

"But what if there's no doctor available or if there's some overwhelming reason why the young man cannot go to a doctor?"

"Well, of course, in that case there are quite a number of things one can do." My mother's eyes lit up. She enjoyed a challenge. "First of all I would take the dried powders of slippery elm and water lily root and make a poultice with warm water for swelling and pain and then . . . ah, any particular reason for asking?"

I hesitated. Of course my secret would be safe with my mother and father, but there was little they could do and they would worry terribly. I was growing up, alas; my parents no longer controlled the universe. No more could they make everything better for me with a hug and a kiss and a juicy mealworm. I was discovering a new world, in which I might suffer and toil and fail and there would be no help for it.

"Those chest wounds wouldn't be gunshot wounds, now would they?" Mother asked anxiously.

"Oh no, nothing like that," I assured her. "These are more like—like the claw marks of a grizzly bear."

"Oh! So, not the sort of thing likely to happen in our neighborhood?" Mother was clearly unsure whether to be puzzled or thankful.

I needed some explanation. I thought for a moment,

with Mother's worried eyes on me. Suddenly I had an inspiration, an idea worthy to be one of Dawn's. In fact it *was* one of Dawn's.

"It's a science project."

"Oh, I see!"

"A history of medicine. What people used when doctors were scarce."

"Yes, of course I see!" My mother laughed in a relieved sort of way. "How very clever of you, darling. You'll write a wonderful report."

"It's not exactly a report," I said, thinking fast. "It's a poster. "I'm going to glue the correct dose of herbs to the poster board and give the proper procedure with drawings. The young man and the grizzly bear are just a made-up case, of course."

"Of course!"

"So I need some help, if you would be so kind."

"How could you doubt it, my love?" said my mother gaily. "Let me see. Your imaginary young man was unfortunate enough to be mauled by a bear and then to get the wounds infected. How high is the fever?"

"I don't know," I said, troubled. "He feels like he's burning up. He's delirious."

Mother shook her head. "That's bad. Tell me, are the wounds swollen and discolored?"

I nodded.

"Are there," she looked very anxiously at me, "any red streaks leading away from the wounds?"

I frowned. "I don't think so," I said.

"Are you sure?"

"Yes, I guess I am."

"Good!" she said, and this time we both laughed, relieved.

"Any nausea, cramps, vomiting?"

"I don't think so. Just the fever and infected wounds."

"Well, then! Now we know where we are. Let's just have a look at what we have in stock, shall we? Hmmm. Ah, here's some comfrey, that's always good, and St.-John's-wort and plantain. Then there are the kitchen herbs . . ." Mother was humming now, absorbed in her task. I felt a little guilty about deceiving her, but the moment for the truth seemed to have passed.

"Could you get some tea down him, do you think? Something to make him sleep and ease the pain."

"I suppose so."

"Sleep is a great healer, darling, especially in this situation."

I nodded and watched while she made up a little bundle of medications and bandages. It would be quite easy to carry the bundle in my beak.

"Is there anything else you haven't told me? Any symptom?"

I thought hard. "Do you have anything," I said slowly, "for insanity?"

"For—insanity?" Mother said doubtfully.

I realized that this might sound a little strange. "Yes," I said quickly. "He was wandering around in the woods for days before he met the bear and it drove him mad." This seemed unlikely even to me.

My mother looked worried again. "Oh dear," she said. "He is an unfortunate young man, isn't he?"

I sighed. "Yes, Mother, he is."

"What sort of insanity is it, exactly? Hysteria? Depression? Schizophrenia?"

"I don't know. The sort that makes you recite poetry to nobody at the top of your lungs and starve yourself for no good reason. The kind that makes your eyes go strange."

"Hysteria, I suppose. He doesn't think he's a rock star or the Pope or anything, does he?"

"Not that I know of."

"Hysteria then, we'll hope." It was her turn to sigh. "Really dear, I hardly know what to suggest. To be quite frank, the old herbal remedies have never been proved entirely effective in this area. To soothe and relax the mind, yes. To cure an illness of the mind—well, I don't know. The tea you already have—I suppose I could add some cowslip and thyme. There's camomile in it already."

She looked so unhappy I leaned forward and hugged her. "I'm sure it will help. Thank you. It means a lot to me."

"I can see that. Tell me, Owl, how do you think Mr. Lindstrom feels about this science project?"

I looked away. "I don't know," I whispered. "I doubt he really cares, one way or another."

"Owl, maybe—"

"Mother, I must go. Thank you and goodbye. Goodbye!" And I hurried from the kitchen.

Clearly my father was already worried, with or without my confidences. When I came upon him unexpectedly in the hall, he screamed. His pale skin turned lilac and his long fingers twisted together anxiously. He seemed on the verge of speech. Then, with a sudden loud bray of laughter, he bolted into the library without a word. A strange way of showing concern, but then he is an unusual and sensitive man.

Twelve

ONCE AGAIN I WAS FLYING hard, back to the north, back to Houle.

When I neared my destination I forced myself to stop, hang my medical bag on a limb, and hunt for my own needs. Owls do not normally spend time commuting to their hunting grounds; they live in their territory and rarely leave it. Flying back and forth from Mr. Lindstrom's neighborhood was already a strain on me. Hunting for two meant pushing myself dangerously hard. The hunting had been excellent this year, but I sensed a change in weather coming. The dry, cold conditions gave every evidence of breaking up into a thaw.

My stomach was almost full when I alighted on the ledge of a window in the Mitchell garage. As I had hoped, Houle slept. He moaned and pushed irritably at the blankets; his fever was still high.

It was as a human that I had to perform the business of the next hour or so. Slipping off the window ledge in human form, I heard a dry twig snap beneath my foot and bit my lip in vexation. Barn owls are famed for the uncanny silence with which they move; humans are not.

I gently cradled Houle in my arms. His lids flipped open momentarily and then closed again. Using an old trick of my mother's, I spooned a paste of ground-up aspirin and puréed grasshoppers into his mouth. He grumbled a bit but swallowed.

Satisfied that he was in no present danger, I hurried away to Mr. Lindstrom's house. It was now 11:30 at night and the house was dark. So far, so good. Still, Mr. Lindstrom had probably only recently retired to bed and might be easily wakened.

I found an outdoor faucet conveniently close to the largest of Houle's gory paintings, but the necessary garden hose was missing, neatly tucked away, waiting for spring. Luckily, the Mitchells kept theirs in the garage.

The plumbing inside Mr. Lindstrom's house made an alarmingly loud rumble as the water rushed to my tap. Working quickly I sprayed methodically up and down the walls of Mr. Lindstrom's house. The stream of water did not work quite as well as I had hoped. Houle's menacing hieroglyphics faded, but a streaky brown outline remained. I watched the upper windows anxiously as I sprayed, but no face appeared; the curtains did not stir.

The hose stretched just far enough to spray down his

next-door neighbor's house as well. Here the marks were confined to a smaller area, and the job was more quickly done. For the next two houses, I simply used handfuls of snow to scrub the marks away.

At the last house, near where Houle had lain, I found a mangled corpse, evidently the source of Houle's paint supply. It was an opossum, I decided. At first I was amazed to think that poor, sick Houle had caught and killed this fierce creature. The fact that it was nearly squashed flat, however, told me that it was road kill; he had merely found it dead by the highway.

I returned to Mr. Lindstrom's house. I was dissatisfied with the way it looked. It was obvious that something had been scribbled here, and a careful eye could pick out the design.

Cautiously I turned the water on to the hose again. One more hosing down could do no harm. In two minutes I was done. The brown streaks remained, but they were faint and indistinct. As I moved to turn the water off, a spotlight suddenly snapped on, flooding the whole area with brilliant white light.

Mr. Lindstrom stood by the back door, holding his bathrobe closed with one hand, his face emotionless, like a mask with two holes cut out of it for eyes.

"What are you doing to my house, Owl?" he asked in

a flat, level voice. He looked unbearably weary, just standing there waiting for my answer.

"I was cleaning it," I managed at last.

"Oh?" He did not offer any comments on this; he simply waited.

"Someone wrote something on it. Something rude. I didn't want you to see it."

"That was very kind of you," he said dryly. It didn't sound as if he thought it was very kind of me. It sounded as if he thought that I was the one who had written something rude on his house and then changed my mind.

"I'm sorry to have wakened you."

"Yes, I imagine you are. Go away, Owl. Turn the water off first. I'll have to report this, you realize. Oh, not to the police," he said, as he saw my stricken look, "but to somebody. I just can't deal with it. Your guidance counselor, I suppose. You can explain it all to her."

I could think of no suitable reply.

"Turn the water off, Owl," Mr. Lindstrom said again. "You're getting your feet all wet."

This was true. I was standing in a very chilly puddle. I turned the water off.

Mr. Lindstrom just stood there staring at me, waiting for me to go.

"Mr. Lindstrom—"

He closed his eyes. "Just go away. Please. I have no idea what you're up to or why. Mrs. Walker will have to handle it. I'm sorry, Owl, but I don't want to think about it, or about you."

This, of course, was the most devastating thing he could possibly have said. Yet I could not help but grieve for him. He looked so tired and sad and . . . to tell the truth, he looked old.

His face was puffy and creased, and a two-day stubble of beard blurred the line of his chin and gave him an untidy look. He had shrunk, somehow, and his back stooped in an elderly curve. His hand was pressed to his stomach as though he had a pain there. Even his voice, that deep golden river of sound that had seduced me again and again, had run as dry and cracked as an empty streambed.

Did I love him any the less? No. Oh, no. Perhaps my love changed in nature, as I stood there looking at him. It evolved into something more mature, a little sadder, a little less adoring. I pitied him from the depths of my heart.

Hesitantly I reached out a cold damp hand and touched his sleeve.

"Good night, Mr. Lindstrom. Sleep well. I hope your dreams bring you some peace."

His eyes snapped open, and he looked at me oddly. "I doubt that, Owl, very much. But thank you. I'll even go so far as to hope you find some sort of peace for yourself too. But not here, Owl; you're going to have to go and find it somewhere else.

"Good night." He gave me a small wan smile. "It's time for me to get back to my dreams, however disquieting they may be. It's very late. Go home and get warm and dry. You'll catch your death." Suddenly he hiccuped. "Excuse me," he said, looking a little embarrassed. "I've got some sort of stomach upset, I'm afraid."

I nodded. Mr. Lindstrom retreated into his house. I watched him go and then turned away myself.

It was a fact that I felt chilled to the bone and so tired that I could have curled up to sleep in the snow like Houle. In owl shape I would snatch a few hours of sleep in a tree before the predawn hunt for Houle's breakfast.

I reluctantly awoke at four o'clock on Friday morning. I shook myself out like a wet feather duster and tried to clear my head for the coming day.

As I had feared, a blanket of clammy clouds hung low to the earth. The damp air slid greasily through my primary feathers as I stretched my wings, preparing for flight.

Owls dislike humidity because it silences the tiny rustles, snaps, and pops that reveal the whereabouts of our prey. You humans would never hear a dry leaf stem compressing under the weight of a rodent's toe, but to an owl that sound is an invitation to dine as loud and as clear as a dinner bell.

I carefully rotated my head, allowing my sensitive ears every chance. Not a sound, except for a gloomy dripping among the trees and an early commuter's car out on the highway.

An hour later I had captured only one mouse and an elderly meadow vole. This would not be enough to satisfy Houle's appetite all the hours I would be at school. Still, it was better than nothing. I collected my bag of medications and flew to Houle.

Doorknobs are awkward things to work in owl shape, so I transformed in order to let myself into the Mitchell garage. I left the two little creatures by Houle's pillow and stood for a moment looking at him, pleased with his deep, regular breathing. He appeared to be profoundly asleep, and for this I was grateful.

His wounds had to be cared for. I unzipped his jacket and unbuttoned his shirt, feeling foolishly shy as I did so. Hot dark blood flooded my neck and cheeks as I lifted his undershirt to inspect his chest.

Why this should be so embarrassing, I could not say. I had already observed his injuries with Dawn; why should it now seem like such a hideously intimate act?

What if Dawn were to come out right now and see me

crouched over him? I stopped and listened intently for sounds of life stirring inside the house.

No, all was well. The Mitchells were not early birds. Early birds? The fantastic image presented itself of Mrs. Mitchell scratching in the garden for worms at dawn like an enormous blond chicken. Human language is beyond understanding sometimes. I returned my attention to Houle's chest.

The wounds were still ugly. I looked carefully for any sign of the red streaks Mother had spoken of. No, the long slashes were puffy and discolored, but there were no other abnormalities.

Very gently I began to apply the herbal salves and healing oils my mother had collected for me, carefully following her instructions. The tips of my fingers discovered that his skin was warm, but not abnormally so; the fever had broken.

When I had finished I gently washed his poor hands and then tidied away the medications. As I straightened his clothing and tucked the blankets around him, I reconsidered my first impression of his appearance. Really, he was not nearly so unattractive as I had thought at our first meeting. He was quite nicely made. His chest muscles were underdeveloped, but he was not unpleasing to look at. In health, and with that something wrong gone from his eyes, I might almost call him good-looking. He was rather undersized for what I took to be his age, but we owl women prefer our men on the small side. It gives us a pleasant sensation of superiority.

I sat back against the wall of the garage and allowed myself to relax for a moment. I had brought along materials to write a brief note to Houle. I suspected that silence and secrecy would be second nature to him, but he might not remember even coming here. Waking in a strange place, he might simply leave.

A delicious drowsiness began to steal over me. How pleasant it would be to close my eyes, just for a moment. Naturally, I was too self-disciplined to do anything of the sort. I would wait just a moment before beginning to write. . . .

I jerked awake to the sound of a ten-year-old male voice bellowing, it seemed, in my ear.

"Ma! Dawn ate all the cereal again! Hey, MA!"

My heart thumping painfully in my throat, I drew out my writing materials and shakily wrote my note. I had slept, I feared, for at least an hour.

"There's no Pop-Tarts or doughnuts or *any*thing!" the child complained.

My dearest Houle,
You are safe. You must not make a sound. The two

girls are your friends. Do what they tell you. Get
as much rest as you can, and I will bring more
food tonight.

Sincerely yours,
Owl

"I'm *hungry!*" wailed the lad. I knew what he meant.

Poor Houle's breakfast looked pitifully small. Nevertheless, I must go, and go quickly. I folded the note and slipped it into his hand, the one that lay under the pillow.

As I let myself quietly out, I heard Mrs. Mitchell's voice raised in reprimand. "Dawn! Dawn, there's not one single thing to eat in this house. Do you hear me, Dawn?"

At least one person would face the day well nourished, anyway.

"Boy, I don't know about that guy," said Dawn two hours later, as she stood conferring with me by my locker.

"Bug OFF, Steve Moran!" I jumped at the savagery in Dawn's voice. She was addressing my neighbor, who appeared to be doing nothing worse than opening his locker, totally ignoring us. "Go hiccup somewhere else. We're talking privately."

Steve Moran did have a very bad case of the hiccups; he'd had them yesterday too. Steve slouched off. Dawn stared after him for a moment, and then continued, "I'm sorry, Owl, but he's really weird. Not Steve," she said irritably, "this Houle person. I mean, I'm pretty broadminded, but I have my limits."

What, I inquired, was the problem?

Dawn did not seem to recognize her good fortune in starting off the day with a full stomach. Her pink brow was creased with worry, and her eyes were troubled. Food isn't everything, unless of course you haven't had any recently.

"You know what I said last night about how he'd poison you just by breathing on you?"

I nodded.

"Well, he did."

"I beg your pardon?"

"I was just kidding when I said it. Or exaggerating, anyway. But when I went out to check on him this morning, there were two dead mice on the pillow next to him. Like they'd run over his pillow in the night, which is kinda creepy in the first place." She shivered. "And then they croaked when they ran into his breath. I guess one of 'em went first and the other one came up to see what was wrong. They were probably husband and wife or something."

Different species, same sex, I wanted to snap, but I couldn't without revealing that it was I who had put them there.

"Maybe it was a suicide pact," Dawn mused, beginning as usual to embroider on the story.

"Mice and voles are promiscuous," I said primly. "There is no marriage bond." I was going to put a stop to this pathetic little drama once and for all.

"Promiscuous? You mean they'll do it with anybody?" Dawn asked, interested.

"That is correct."

"So what's a vole?"

"Very similar to a mouse, but with a short tail and rounder features," I explained.

"That sounds like one of those mice this morning," Dawn said suspiciously. "How did you know?"

I shrugged. "Hu— I mean, *people* often confuse the two." I nearly said "humans."

"Hmm," Dawn said. "Anyway, I felt sorry for the poor little things. They're so cute."

I drew myself up. "A single female mouse can give birth to one hundred and thirty mice in a three-year lifetime. Mice breed at the age of six weeks. If every one of those one hundred and thirty mice and *their* offspring survived, within three years that mother mouse would have a family numbering in the millions. The descendants of that one mouse would swarm over the earth, devouring everything in their path. Life as we know it would come to a halt."

Dawn appeared somewhat taken aback. I had spoken passionately, I knew, and at much greater length than usual.

"Well," she said. "I didn't know that."

"Without constant control by predators we would be literally knee-deep in rodents. Artificial methods of extermination are hopelessly inadequate. And by destroying habitats where rodent predators live, we are preparing a present-day town of Hamelin for ourselves. I doubt very much that a Pied Piper will appear to save us."

"Huh?" said Dawn. "Town of Hamelin?"

"Surely you have heard of 'The Pied Piper of Hamelin'? The rats that 'fought the dogs and killed the cats, and bit the babies in the cradles'? Robert Browning?"

"Oh. Um, maybe. So you figure one or two dead mice isn't such a tragedy, huh?"

"No, indeed."

"Well, okay. But they *are* cute, I don't care what you say, Owl. And why did they die right there, next to his face?"

"Perhaps he killed them as they chewed on his clothing, and was too weak to push them away."

"Maybe," Dawn said doubtfully.

The bell rang at that moment, and we moved apart to our respective classes.

"He gives me the *creeps*, Owl," Dawn called after me.

Thirteen

I ALLOWED DAWN TO CARRY me off unresisting on the school bus again after school. I would far rather have been free to hunt, but it was difficult to deny Dawn anything when she was risking so much for Houle and me.

But it seemed that she wanted me only as an audience for her complaints about Houle.

"He probably picked the lock on the garage door and spent the day in the house," she muttered darkly. "I bet he knows how. They must teach 'em something in reform school."

"I don't think it was a reform—"

"Probably raided the refrigerator and slept all day in one of the beds. Ugh! I hope it wasn't mine."

She brooded on this possibility all the way to her house. "Whaddya wanta bet he stripped the cupboard shelves right down to the finish? Not that there's anything to eat, anyway."

Dawn paused with her hand on the garage door.

"Maybe he isn't there," she suggested hopefully. "What if he woke up and felt better and decided to leave because he knew he might get us into a lot of trouble? I mean, maybe?"

I shook my head.

"Well, okay, it was just a thought."

Houle had managed to make himself almost invisible, but he was there all right. Nothing but a mud-colored cheek and a lock of greasy hair protruded from what appeared to be a pile of dirty laundry in the corner. He was sleeping peacefully.

Dawn disappeared to inspect the state of the kitchen and then returned, gnawing on some hoarded delicacy. She watched critically as I tended to his wounds.

"What's that? It smells like the art room at school."

"Linseed oil to dress his wounds," I explained.

"Oil? You're dressing him with oil? What do you think he is, a tossed salad?" She sniffed. "Frankly, I like my greens a little fresher. You wouldn't let me try out the stuff in our medicine cabinet on him, but you're greasing him up with that junk? At least ours is real medicine."

"My mother recommended it."

"Hunh!" she said. "A magic potion, I suppose."

"Well, no—"

"Magic spells, love potions, huh! Buncha garbage." I was rather surprised by her air of bitter disillusionment, as though she'd just found out that the tooth fairy was making a killing selling black market baby molars.

"Oh well," she said discontentedly. She stared gloomily at Houle for a few moments, and then asked: "Did your mom know who the grease was for?"

Startled, I shook my head no.

"Don't you think she's got a right to know?"

"You didn't tell your mother, and he's staying in your garage," I said defensively.

"Yeah, but that's different."

I had to agree. It seemed to me that Mrs. Mitchell had a much better claim than Mrs. Tycho.

"It isn't right, Owl," she said, shaking her head at me. "Their own son."

"Daughter," I corrected gently. Dawn was getting mixed up. The strain was clearly too much for her.

"Wha-at? Daughter!" She turned her gaze from me back to Houle. "That," she said, "is a boy."

"Certainly," I agreed.

"Well, then—"

"And I am a girl," I added helpfully.

Dawn made a snarling noise. "I know that. You're a girl and your rotten brother's a boy. Unless of course we're all just figments of our own imagination."

"No, no," I said soothingly. "Wait—my what?"

"Your brother, the howling hyena here."

"But—I have no brother."

"Whaddya mean you haven't got a brother? You guys

could be twins. Sure! Owl and Houle. Just the kind of dumb rhyming names twins get." She stared wildly back and forth from Houle to me. "You are! You must be twins! Don't you ever look at yourself in the mirror?"

She had me there. I don't often, because we do not own one and I don't like using strange bathrooms. The makeup session was the first time in a year or two.

"Rarely," I admitted.

She clutched her head melodramatically. "It figures. Take it from me, you two are like a black dog and its own shadow."

"Well!" I said, feeling faintly injured. Although of late I had begun to change my mind, I had from the beginning considered Houle a rather unattractive creature.

"Sure," she said excitedly. "Look. Same flat, broad cheekbones, same heart-shaped face, same enormous eyes. His are black and yours yellow but basically identical. And here—" She grabbed my wrist and laid my hand on his arm. "See? Almost the exact same skin color. His is a little browner, but close. A lot closer than any of those skin tones in that magazine, that's for sure."

"Hmm," I said, not wishing to commit myself.

"And you claim he's not your brother?"

I nodded.

"No relation at all?"

I shook my head.

"Baloney! He must be!"

"Not to my knowledge, Dawn."

Dawn was silent for a moment, looking intently at Houle.

"Then why are we protecting him?"

The question hit me like a blow to the stomach. This was why Dawn had helped. She had been so understanding because she had misunderstood. Now what? Would she agree to hide him when she realized that he was nothing more than a pet boy?

"Because . . . because he needs me—us."

Dawn frowned. "No. He needs somebody, maybe, but there are lots of other people better equipped to give him what he needs. He'd be better off with doctors and—no offense—real medicine."

I felt a disagreeable sensation in my wrists and down my spine. It was my blood, I realized, running cold in my veins. I made an instinctive movement with my arms, warding Dawn away from Houle. Dawn folded her arms and did not stir.

"I'm not afraid of you, Owl," she said. "At least I am, kind of, when your eyes go like that, but you have to listen to sense. I could see you going all out to protect your brother from the loony bin, but a total stranger? You haven't got the *right* to deny this guy medical care if he's just a . . . a—"

"A hobby?" I suggested miserably.

"Yeah, right, a hobby. So what is this guy to you, anyway?"

I groaned and bowed my head.

"Okay, I see he means a lot to you. But you have to give him up. I mean it, Owl. You have to turn him in. It isn't fair. Not to him and not . . . not to me, either."

A long silence, while we listened to each other breathing.

"I can't."

Dawn made a gesture of impatience.

"I can't, Dawn. Please don't ask me," I whispered. "Please."

"Oh, hell," she said disgustedly.

Neither of us spoke for a moment.

"I guess you won't stay for dinner, huh?" Dawn said at last. "You won't eat any of our food, will you? No, I didn't think so. Don't you like our food, or don't you like people to see you eat?"

Alarmed by the nature of this new question, I simply stood there and looked at her.

"All of the above, huh? You don't like our food and you don't want anybody to see what you do eat. Or how you eat. You must have some gross table manners."

I ignored the insult. I would far rather she thought I

drooled or belched at the table than realize how close her guesses were coming.

"And you won't let me feed or nurse him." She jerked her head in Houle's direction. "You don't want me to see what he eats either, do you? I haven't seen you feeding him, but I bet you have. You wouldn't let him go this long without food. He didn't eat anything from the refrigerator today."

I watched her warily and said nothing.

"And while I'm in there eating SpaghettiOs at the dinner table, you'll be out getting the two of you whatever it is you do eat, right?"

I really did not know what to say.

"Right?"

Seeing that she would not let me off without an answer, I nodded my head very slightly, yes.

She grunted, then sighed.

"You're not used to being friends with anybody, are you, Owl?" was the next, unexpected question. I shook my head, no.

"I can tell."

I felt someone watching me as I left the garage. When I looked back, I saw Dawn's round face in the living room window. I had planned to cut around through her back yard to the woods and transform there, but this was clearly not practical under Dawn's baleful gaze.

I trudged off down the street as though headed home. Just outside of the development a narrow finger of trees reached out from the woods and touched the main road. Out of Dawn's sight, I could casually turn aside into this little corridor between field and suburb and soon find myself some privacy.

How slow and wearisome this walking was! I longed to spread my wings and lift up over the rooftops, freeing myself from this tight, tidy place of straight lines and right angles. Plod, plod, plod, one foot in front of the other.

The day was still moist and clammy, with none of the hard-edged clarity dear to an owl's heart. February was going all soft and runny around the edges, melting into March. Crisp, cold hunting nights would come more rarely now. The rains of spring were on the move, chilling heart and bone, stealing the prey from our bellies. Perhaps I could teach Houle to hunt a little for himself. How would a human catch a mouse? How had my parents taught me?

My parents. Dawn was right, if for the wrong reasons. I must tell them about Houle. Dawn could not be trusted much longer. Somehow I had to get Houle to my house, where he could be cared for properly.

I considered the idea of a taxi. I had no money, or any

idea what it would cost. Could I get Houle into the taxi without the Mitchells' knowing? Would Dawn inform the authorities?

My parents would help. They wouldn't know how much a cab cost, but they would almost certainly insist upon paying for it out of household expense money.

It was this last that troubled me. I knew, none better, how hard that money was come by. Last week the roof over the kitchen had developed a leak and needed expensive repairs. My parents and I (if I could find the time in my frantic schedule) would do the work and find many of the materials at the town dump. Still, some supplies would have to be purchased, using money intended for other purposes.

My good, gentle-hearted parents would never hesitate. "Of course we must save your friend," my darling father would say. And my mother: "A hole in the roof? So convenient!" she would insist. "Right in the kitchen, too. When it's raining I can fill my kettle just by pushing it under the hole. Very useful, darling."

But that was all kindly nonsense. The hole in the roof would grow bigger, and soon the whole ceiling would cave in. The housing inspector would come to hear about it, and the next thing you knew, there we would be, out in the street. The hole in the roof must be fixed.

How does one get money in a hurry? The usual jobs

undertaken by teens did not seem practical to me. Baby-sitting? I did not know one end of a human baby from the other. Mowing lawns? The wrong season. Shoveling snow? It had not snowed in two weeks. Besides, I simply did not have the time for any of this. I was considering the possibility of a short-term crime spree when I was interrupted.

"Hey! (Hic!) Owl Tycho! Is that you?"

Immediately all dishonorable thoughts of lonely gas stations and all-night markets fled from my brain. That was Mr. Lindstrom's voice.

"Owl! It is you." He had pulled his car off to the side of the road and was motioning me over to him. With a now-familiar sense of guilt, I realized I had forgotten all about him, and about the house-washing incident last night. Even—I gulped—that I was supposed to report to Mrs. Walker today.

"Did you talk to Mrs. Walker?" he asked immediately, as though reading my mind.

"Ah, no. I thought she would call me in," I lied.

"That's right. Good (hic). I didn't tell her. I had a look at the marks on the house (hic). You did a pretty good job, but you didn't quite get them all off. Owl, (hic) listen. I believe you. I don't think you made those marks. But (hic) I need to know. This is very important, Owl. Did you see who did make them (hic)?"

I am not the sort of person who finds ordinary bodily

functions hysterically funny. Still, it was hard to keep a straight face and concentrate on what Mr. Lindstrom was saying through this storm of hiccuping. I am sorry to say that the fact that he seemed so very much in earnest made the effect even more comical.

I tried to pull myself together. This was serious. What was I to answer? I tried a diversion.

"You could drink out of the wrong side of a glass for those hiccups," I suggested helpfully.

Mr. Lindstrom gestured irritably. "Never mind the hiccups (hic!). I don't know what's causing them. Stress, probably. But who made those drawings on the house, Owl? Who? (Hic!) Did you see?"

Didn't Mr. Lindstrom start hiccuping last night, at the end of our conversation? "You were hiccuping last night," I said. Mr. Lindstrom hadn't been drinking to forget his troubles. His breath smelled faintly of pizza.

"Yes! (Hic!) All right. I was hiccuping last night! I'm having a world-class hiccup attack. It hasn't let up for eighteen hours (hic). I don't care about the hiccups. I want to know who you saw writing on my house. You saw somebody, didn't you? That's why (hic) you keep talking about hiccups."

With sudden relief I realized that I didn't have to lie.

"Mr. Lindstrom," I said solemnly. "I didn't see who made those marks."

He stared at me, baffled. Then he said, "Yes, but you know who made them, don't you?"

Oh, crafty Mr. Lindstrom! Now I was back in the same fix as before.

"I didn't see anybody," I repeated stubbornly.

"Hic!" Mr. Lindstrom began to tap his fingers on the side of the car. I could tell that he was longing for a notebook to tear. He fixed me with a piercing gaze.

"Why do I feel, Owl, that you know something (hic) that you aren't telling? Look, this is important. It's more important than you could possibly know (hic)."

I knew just how important it was. It was Mr. Lindstrom who could not understand the importance of the issue. Did he suspect that it was the escaped mental patient who had made the marks? He must.

"Owl, come over to my house for a minute (hic). I'd like to talk to you about this. If you're trying to shield—" He broke off, biting his lip. He leaned over and pushed the door on the passenger side open. "Would you? (Hic.) Just for a few minutes?"

Oh dear. I had to feed Houle, and I did not think I could bear to be grilled by Mr. Lindstrom on this subject.

"Well—"

"Please!" he said urgently. "I mean it, Owl, I'm begging you (hic)."

After that, of course, I had no choice. I got in.

As we drove off, I noticed a strange tree. It was strange both because of its shape, which was remarkably plump and curvy near the base, and because of its behavior. Most trees hardly have any behavior to speak of. They grow and they bend in the wind and that's about it. This tree seemed to be shifting its weight from one root to another as though it were tired of standing all the time in one position.

Surprised, I twisted around in my seat to look at it again, but this time it looked quite normal. It was as slender and well behaved as any suburban beech tree I've ever seen.

The drive was naturally very short, and Mr. Lindstrom seemed to be holding his fire until we were actually under his roof. For this I was very grateful.

It suddenly occurred to me that I was about to enter Mr. Lindstrom's actual home. A few short weeks ago that would have been almost more bliss than I could bear. Now I found the adventure remarkably flat. I was too worried to spare more than a brief distracted thought for the delights I was about to experience.

We pulled into the driveway. Dully, I noticed the presence of another car, with out-of-state plates. We walked up the path, and Mr. Lindstrom stood for a moment fishing his house key out of his pocket.

Before he could fit it into the lock, the door swung

wide open. The Wailing Woman stood there, and she was at it again.

"John! John!" she wailed, like a lost soul falling eternally through the abyss.

I looked behind us. John? Who was this John she was calling? Perhaps she was a ghost after all, and she was crying out to her demon lover.

"What's the matter, darling?"

I turned my head, unbelieving. These terrible words had issued from the mouth of my love, my future husband, Mr. Lindstrom. He went on.

"Sweetheart, tell me, what is it? (Hic!) What's happened now?"

"John, they've found something."

In front of my horrified eyes, Mr. Lindstrom enfolded the Wailing Woman in his arms and bent her head to his shoulder. He stroked her hair and hissed at her like a trainer soothing a skittish horse. "Ssss, now, it's all right," he whispered, staring sightlessly over her head.

All my internal organs, most notably my heart, slowly shriveled, crumbled to dust, and blew away.

"It's going to be okay, baby. Everything's going to be fine. (Hic!) Hush, now hush." The Wailing Woman paid no attention to this sensible advice, but yowled louder than ever. Mr. Lindstrom joined the chorus, mumbling broken endearments between hiccups into her hair. They had obviously both forgotten my very existence.

"Please don't cry, sweetie."

"Oooohh, John—!"

(Hic!) "Don't cry, little love."

"Ohhhh . . ."

(Hic!)

I turned and ran away as hard as I could into the wood.

Fourteen

As I ran, the sun sank below the horizon. Like my heart, the earth grew cold. The wet snow stiffened and crusted over, and every step I took was a dragging, plunging misery. It was like one of those dreary nightmares in which you flee from an enemy with bags of cement strapped to your ankles. I felt physically ill. My hands trembled like aspen leaves in a gale, my throat burned with a rising tide of vomit. I wanted to weep and to break something and to lie down and go to sleep all at the same time.

When I think back on that terrible moment I cannot believe I managed to remain in human form until I was at least partially shielded from view in the forest. The moment I stepped under the sheltering trees I spread my arms and, with a wild, anguished scream, took to the sky.

Transformed to an owl, my emotions simplified. I was angry and I wanted to kill. I found by sheer instinct. I nailed mice with the swift, merciless precision of a hammer. One, two, three, four, five, and then six, seven, eight. I gulped down the first five; my enormous anger required fuel. The next three I hid in a tree near Dawn's house and went hunting for more.

When I had six mice in my stash, I flew to Dawn's garage. I tapped on the windowpane with my beak. In a moment, Houle's face looked back at me, like a reflection in a mirror. Dawn was right, as she was right about so many things. We are alike, Houle and I.

I could see that he was free from fever, but still very weak. When he saw me and, still more, the mice dangling from my beak, his eyes brightened. It took all his strength to lift the stiff window sash, but at last he managed it, and I hopped inside.

He quickly swallowed the mice and then whispered, "Owl, I have to go away. It's too dangerous . . ." He trailed off and then stared wretchedly at me. "You don't understand me, do you? How could you? Although—" He broke off and regarded me with troubled black eyes. He fumbled in his jacket and pulled out the note I had written to him. After a moment he shrugged his shoulders and muttered, "It was just a joke by those girls, that's all. How could he have written that note?"

He thought I was a male! Insulted, my feathers ruffled up indignantly, and I hissed at him.

Houle drew back a little. "Sorry," he said, his eyes big and scared. "Then . . . you mean you did write that note? You understand English?"

This conversation was getting too complicated. Confused, I did not react quickly enough. I simply stared at him.

Houle's face changed with bewildering speed. His eyes lost their focus, and the muscles around his mouth went loose and flabby. "No, 'course not. Only a crazy boy'd think that. Crazy boy," he mumbled. His voice slurred as though he could not be bothered to form the words properly. "You're crazed in your wits, stupid boy, lazy boy, nasss-ty boy." He laughed, on a high, cracked note. "'It was the owl that shrieked, the fatal bellman . . . it is a knell that summons thee to heaven or to hell—' Ow! Hey, stop that!"

I had bitten him on the hand to stop the monotonous falsetto. He did sound crazy when he talked like that. The quotation was from *Macbeth*, reading material far too gloomy for a sensitive boy with a mind in delicate balance. If he must read Shakespeare, surely the comedies would be a better choice.

"That hurts," he said sulkily, but I was pleased to see that his eyes were sharp and his speech clear. "I'm freezing," he complained, and shut the window.

"'This cold night will turn us all to fools and madmen,'" I responded promptly. When people get to trading quotes from Mr. Shakespeare, I am not often at a loss. Naturally it was wasted on Houle. He did not understand me.

"What do I do now, Owl?" he asked.

This was rather awkward. Now that he had shut the window I was rather wondering what I was to do myself.

I decided to transform in front of him. This was a reckless decision. He had just demonstrated that his sanity was not to be relied upon. Yet I wanted to prove to him and to myself that I trusted him and thought him worthy to keep my secret. I wanted to put myself in his power. Mr. Lindstrom's betrayal had made me hungry for reassurance. I needed to believe in someone.

He had flung himself down on the modified dog bed and was staring at me in a hopeless, dejected kind of way. His eyes grew suddenly round, however, as my form wavered and misted before him. He sat up.

"Owl—!"

I couldn't do it. A cold fear nibbled at my stomach. I beat my wings, groping for arms, for human hands. My heart and mind remained fierce and wild; I was filled to the brim with owl thoughts and owl feelings. The terror spread, coursing through my veins like some dark, maddening wine. I hissed like a dragon, like a teakettle on the boil. Houle cowered in his corner, infected with my panic.

Never had I so longed for my own humanity. I wanted skin and hair and dirty tennis shoes, not feathers, beak, and claws. In my frenzy I hardly noticed Houle crawling toward the window.

"Wait! wait!" he panted. With a grunt he thrust it open and flung himself to the floor, out of reach of my slashing talons. He whimpered with pain as he hit, but I was too maddened with fear to notice. I gripped the sill, turning my head to look at him where he lay on the floor.

In this strange state, trying so fiercely to transform, I found an almost human voice.

"S-s-stay," I croaked. "S-s-sleep. Be s-silent."

I could not tell if he understood. His jaw dropped, and his eyes were shocked and huge, so perhaps he did. I flew away into the night, for the first time truly a prisoner in my body.

I went home. It seemed the most sensible thing to do. I flew into my own open window and then downstairs into the kitchen and sat on my mother's chair.

"Owl! You haven't changed over! What is the matter?"

There were so many answers to this that no answer was possible.

"Owl! Please, you're worrying me. Do transform."

I tried. Mother watched attentively as I tried.

"Oh, my poor darling, what has happened to you? Something terrible, I can see that."

I nodded, or tried, but owls do not nod easily. Mother understood, as I knew she would.

"Was it Mr. Lindstrom? Or—the other one?"

I groaned. Both, it was both! The two of them were tearing my heart and soul to rags between them, like puppies playing with an old sock. I noticed that Mother did not believe in my fiction about the science project. I would never be as good a liar as Dawn.

I was saved the trouble of trying to answer by the entrance of my father. He shied like a horse at the sight of me, then recovered.

"Oh, hello there, Owl," he said, baring big, yellow teeth at me.

"Stop grinning and nodding your head at the girl like that," snapped my mother. "What on earth's the matter with you? Can't you see she's in a terrible fix? Her heart is broken, and now she can't find her way back to human shape."

"No!" said my father, obviously horrified.

"Yes!"

"Please, Nesta, say it isn't true," he begged.

"Why should I, when it is true, as true as can possibly be?"

My father suddenly burst into loud sobs. I was rather surprised. I felt somewhat uneasy about my condition, but I had no doubt that I would eventually be able to remedy it.

"I never meant to k-kill him. I didn't, please believe me! I didn't know, not for sure, that it was even him! Oh, I'm so sorry, Owl! Can you ever forgive me?"

He certainly had our attention now.

"Frederich Tycho! Explain yourself!" my mother commanded, drawing herself up with a look like thunder. "Kill whom?"

"Oh, that dratted science teacher, of course! That Mr. Lindstrom. It shouldn't have hurt him at all, not really. I never thought—"

I struggled for utterance, but nothing would come save an outraged hiss. My mother spoke for me.

"What have you done to him, Frederich?"

"Nothing much. Do you mean he isn't dead? When you said Owl had broken her heart, I thought—"

"Frederich!"

"It was that girl! That yellow-haired girl! It was her fault. She mumbles. If she'd only spoken more clearly there wouldn't have been a mix-up."

A yellow-haired girl?

"What girl, Fritz?" Mother asked patiently.

"Dawn, she said her name was. She came here one day last week when you were out, dear, and asked me for some glove lotion. At least that's what I thought she said."

Dawn? Glove lotion?

"Dawn? Glove lotion? Do you mean that girl Owl had for a lab partner?"

"I suppose so. Yes, I admit it. I knew it was her, really.

Oh, Owl, please forgive me. It was only that I'm a little hard of hearing."

"First I've heard of it," my mother said. "Come now, Fritz, you must tell us. What is this all about? What does glove lotion have to do with Mr. Lindstrom?"

"I suppose he drank it, or ate it," said my father miserably.

I gave a sort of croaking cry, and my mother gasped. "Fritz! What have you done? Why? Why would he eat or drink it?"

"Well, at first I thought she was asking me for glove lotion. I gave her that, but then I thought maybe it was really a love potion she wanted. I—I fear I was somewhat confused at the time. I gave her the glove lotion and the instructions for the love potion. She said it was for him."

Confusion settled on my brain like a thick yellow fog. I couldn't imagine why Dawn should give Mr. Lindstrom a love potion. She surely wasn't in love with him herself? She had been so anxious to help! And she was my friend, wasn't she?

"Fritz, you old fool! Don't you see what you've done!" My mother's voice was bitter, and we flinched. She turned on him, her body rigid with anger.

"Because of your stupid jealousy, you have ruined us in this town! Will they come to us anymore, these good people, when they hear what you have done? Of course not! Would you? Would anyone with a grain of sense? What was in that glove lotion?"

I was anxious to hear that also.

"It—it was a simple spell to keep kid gloves white, that's all. Ladies don't wear white kid gloves much any-more, so we hardly ever sell it. Oh, Nesta, please don't hate me. I never meant to hurt him. Perhaps—listen, Nesta, perhaps he never had any. Or perhaps he did but is still perfectly well. It was an old preparation, and weak besides."

"Oh, Fritz!"

"It should only have made him hiccup. And perhaps given him a bit of indigestion. That is all, I swear it. I thought—I thought that if Owl had to hear that 'golden voice' of his through a steady stream of hiccups, it would take away some of his fatal glamour. I thought—oh I don't know what I thought. It was all just on the spur of the moment. There has not been a moment since when I have not regretted it."

I closed my eyes. Yes, Mr. Lindstrom had eaten some. If only hiccups and indigestion were the sole results! Please let them be. Please.

My mother sighed. "Fritz, I love you; I cannot help myself. It is my doom. Come, we will put our heads together and find a way to cure this poor man. Owl, go to sleep. Perhaps when you wake, the world will look a little better than it does now."

Gloomily, I flew back to my room and settled down for a nap on the bedpost. I did not see how anything was going to look much better any time in the near future.

Dawn. My first and only friend. Had she then been my rival the whole time? No wonder she had questioned me so closely about Mr. Lindstrom. She was spying out my feelings, trying to guess whether or not she had a chance herself. Why else should she care so much?

Examined in this light, her behavior assumed a very different appearance. She had tried to discourage me in my love, suggesting Mr. Lindstrom could never return it. She hinted that my passion was weak and wavering. She made up foolish stories to discredit Mr. Lindstrom and tried to shift my attention to another, lesser male.

The afternoon spent applying cosmetics: could all that have been part of her plot? Instead of beautifying me, she had painted me orange and then sent me home just in time to encounter Mr. Lindstrom. What had she not done to separate us, while pretending to try to unite us?

But why had she consented to shelter Houle, if she was in reality my enemy? Perhaps it pleased her to have me too busy for Mr. Lindstrom. However I shook the tangle, it would not hang straight.

This thing, "friendship," is nothing but a handsome

mask to hide the sneer of a traitor. "Friendship is constant in all other things save in the office and affairs of love." Shakespeare, as usual, had had something to say on the subject.

I had *liked* the girl. Damn Shakespeare! Why couldn't he just hold his tongue? Everyone seemed against me. I faced betrayal on every side. Dawn, my own father, Mr. Lindstrom.

Oh, Mr. Lindstrom! My mind went back to those ghastly moments on the Lindstrom steps, watching as my chosen mate nuzzled and fondled another, right before my very eyes.

His name was John. It had never occurred to me that he might have another name. Never had I addressed him in my most intimate imaginings as anything but "Mr. Lindstrom."

John Lindstrom.

Didn't it sound, well, a little ordinary? Just a bit dull? Was that the name of a wereowl's husband?

On the edge of sleep, my mind slid away from John Lindstrom and returned to Houle. Houle, my wild boy, my burden, my sweet obsession. He at least was true to me.

I slept. So exhausted was I that I did not wake in an hour or two as usual. It was nine o'clock in the morning when I opened my eyes. My mother had let me sleep. I yawned and stretched my wings, glad she had allowed it. I felt a little groggy but better than I had in days. I could not have gone to school looking as I did, anyway. I was still emphatically in owl form. I tried to transform, but only halfheartedly. I could tell it was no use.

My stomach growled. I had had nothing to eat all night after feeding Houle.

Houle! Not only would he be terribly hungry, but he was possibly in great danger. If Dawn was a false friend, I could not trust her a moment longer.

Where was I to take him? I could not, even if I wished to, involve my parents. The idea of trying to explain about Houle, his desperate plight, his present location, and a plan of rescue with a hiss and a squawk and one or two gestures of the head, depressed me.

Could he possibly manage to walk here by himself, on his own two legs? He was growing stronger. At least we could get him out of the garage, into the shelter of the woods. If we took it very, very slowly, resting every half hour . . . ?

I didn't know. I didn't know if it would be wise. Certainly he had improved, but it was only thirty-six hours since he had been raving with fever.

At least I must get him away from Dawn's house. I would go now, right away. Mother would understand why

I did not bid her goodbye. As for Father—I wasn't sure I wanted to see him yet. It was all very well for Mother to forgive him; she was married to him. It would take me a little while longer.

I lunged off the bedpost, where I had roosted for the night, and flew out the window.

Fifteen

DAWN'S HEAD BOBBED ALONG below me, a yellow oval against the blue-gray asphalt road. We were approaching Mr. Lindstrom's house, she walking and I flying. I would have found it difficult to keep to her slow pace, except that I was nearly paralyzed with hatred.

The appearance of that particular blond head had been a source of some amazement to me when I first spotted it moving steadily along Harvest Hill Road. It was 9:45 in the morning, time for third period at Wildewood Senior High School. Why was she here rather than there?

It took me less than a minute—thirty seconds, perhaps—to comprehend the full extent of her wickedness. From the shelter of a young maple tree in Mr. Lindstrom's front yard, I watched my faithless friend as she mounted the steps and rang the bell. I understood her. Oh yes, I understood her only too well now.

Mr. Lindstrom's white, unhappy face appeared. He looked puzzled. Why, he no doubt asked, was Dawn not in school? Her pink lips moved. She spoke very low, and I could not hear what she said. I was too far away to make out distinct words. I did not need to; I knew what she was telling him.

Mr. Lindstrom's face changed, rather as Houle's had, last night. His whole face went blank. The lines around his mouth and eyes vanished. He looked remote, like a doll, or an infant in the cradle.

He grabbed Dawn's shoulder, as if to steady himself. I envied her that touch, though I saw her wince in pain. She did not protest but stood silent while he gathered himself together.

After a moment, he turned and looked back into the house. He did not speak but seemed to be thinking hard. Then he shook his head, not at Dawn but at his own thoughts. He stepped out of his doorway, coatless, bootless, ready to follow wherever Dawn should lead him. It was Dawn who closed the door behind him, frowning at his carelessness.

Strictly speaking, I did not know that I had any right to complain. I had certainly used Dawn's ideas often enough in the past few days without a twinge of guilt. Dawn had simply been more thorough than I. Not only had she taken my idea, but she proposed to steal away from me both Mr. Lindstrom and my wild boy, Houle, at one fell swoop.

She even seemed to have taken over the scene I had imagined, in which I led Mr. Lindstrom to Houle's hiding place. It took place at midmorning, not at night, and their walk led them through suburban streets rather than woodland, but otherwise it was the same. He even stumbled once on the crust of snow, and she reached out her hand and caught his arm.

He walked as though in a trance. No admiring or friendly looks were thrown her way, and my heart was glad to see it. For all her lies and deceit, Dawn's pursuit of Mr. Lindstrom seemed no likelier than mine to succeed. Far better the Wailing Woman should have him than Dawn, if I could not.

I followed them only a moment, to try and overhear a word, a phrase, to guess what they were likely to do. Then I had to hurry to Houle and warn him. I flew dangerously close, trying to catch their voices as they were blown away on the wind. Dawn looked up, surprised.

"What was that?" she said. "I saw something."

Mr. Lindstrom did not even bother to look. He just repeated his question. ". . . say he's ill? What's wrong?"

Dawn murmured something in reply.

"Injured? How badly?"

Dawn shook her head and tugged on his shirt sleeve, to hurry him along. I left them then. However slowly they walked, Houle would be slower, and they would search for him in the woods, if they did not find him in the garage or house.

How I longed to transform! I could not explain half of what needed to be said in my present form, and speed was essential. I tapped with my beak against the window. Houle was there, huddled under a blanket, barely visible, but he did not move. He was deeply asleep. I rapped again, sharply. He did not respond.

I imagined for a moment that I could hear the crunch of footsteps on snow approaching. Terrified, I lifted off the windowsill and then turned in the air to dash myself against the windowpane. With a thud! and a crack! I was through, bleeding about the head but still mercifully conscious. Dizzily I surveyed the room. Houle was sitting up in bed with a blanket clutched to his chin like an old maid in a cartoon.

"Owl!" he cried softly. He looked almost afraid of me.

I flapped my wings at him and hissed as expressively as I could, but he just sat there gaping at me, looking about as lively as a hard-boiled egg.

Nearly shrieking with exasperation, I rushed at him, beak open. Owls run very badly. Our talons are made for grasping, not for speed on the ground. On the other hand, this was a small space. Houle was up and out of bed and then out of the door in a moment. I chased him out of the garage, out into the snow.

I would have felt pleased at this success, but he was

not being as quiet as I could wish. It was not in his nature to shout, but he was hissing and sputtering protests in a very loud whisper: "Stop it! What are you doing? Don't touch me!" and so on, as he ran. He was also, I noted to my dismay, in stocking feet and jacketless. Never mind. I had to have him out of there. Dawn and Mr. Lindstrom would be there in minutes.

I herded him, as best I could, toward the woods. As we ran I tried to confuse his footsteps in the snow by brushing them with my wings, but the glaze of ice made this very difficult. We might as well have left a trail of bread crumbs for them to follow.

In another moment the treacherous ice dealt us another blow. Houle tripped and fell headlong into the snow. I turned and flew directly at him.

"No, Owl, no!" he cried, not troubling to lower his voice at all. He threw up an arm to ward me off, but of course it was not my intention to harm him. I flew off and sat in a nearby tree, to allow him to get to his feet again. When he did, I launched myself at him again, flying perilously close to his head, making irritated grinding noises with my beak. He promptly sat down in the snow again.

I quickly calmed my anger. I summoned up from within myself a vast patience. I reminded myself that he was still very weak, that he had just been wakened from a deep sleep, that I was behaving in an apparently threatening and certainly alarming way. I would not think about Dawn and Mr. Lindstrom, now only seconds away.

If I could not drive him, I would lead him. I flew by him again, this time more slowly, and not so close. I landed in the same tree and made what I hoped were encouraging noises.

"What do you want, Owl? What?" he quavered, from his seat on the icy ground.

Pleased by the question, I flew slowly on, to a small conifer a few feet closer to the woods. There I stopped and looked back at him.

"Huh?" he said stupidly. I sighed.

"Where're you going, Owl?" He sounded distressed now, as though afraid of being abandoned. I stood still, hoping against hope. He staggered to his feet and stood looking after me. I fluttered my feathers, as though making ready to fly. He took a step toward me. Then another.

"There he is!" came Dawn's excited voice, alarmingly close. There they were, not a hundred feet away, rounding the garage. I had hoped for a few more minutes while they searched the house, but it was not to be. They had seen us, or rather, they had seen Houle.

Houle turned and saw them.

To my sudden horror, I realized that Houle did not know Dawn was his enemy, that she meant to turn him over to the authorities. I myself had instructed him to trust her.

Mr. Lindstrom overtook Dawn, pushing past her. Everyone moved slowly, awkwardly, through the iced-over snow, so that the entire scene was made up of lurching, clumsy actors, stumbling toward one another, gesturing wildly, and fighting to keep their balance.

"David!" Mr. Lindstrom cried, his voice and figure both tiny in the bright white yard. I noticed that he was still hiccuping.

Houle seemed puzzled at being so addressed. He paused. I felt a pain, like a skewer inserted between my ribs. I actually looked down to inspect my wound before I realized the injury was to my soul, not to my skin.

"David, please! It's me!" Mr. Lindstrom had jerked his way a little closer.

"It's okay, Houle," cried Dawn. Then, with a treachery that took my breath away, she said, "Owl wants you to come with us. We'll take care of you."

Houle swiveled his head back around to me.

"No!" I said. "No no no!" But of course he did not understand me.

"David! Your mother! She's here! She wants to see you. She's terribly worried about you." Mr. Lindstrom hiccuped.

Houle's gaze shifted. He scanned the area, looking for this mythical mother.

"No, not here, at the house. Come back with me to the house."

It was so cruel I did not know how I could bear it. To try and trick him like that, tempting him with a mother who had sent him away! Even if it was true, even if—my mind made a sudden leap—the Wailing Woman. Could she be the mother?

So that woman who had cast him off when his poor wits had gone wandering wanted him now, did she? If he had been mine I would never have allowed him to run mad, no I would not!

Houle was turning toward him, leaning toward Mr. Lindstrom, like a tall pine tree in a high wind. He wanted her, wanted her love so badly that he would tear his very roots from the good earth, rip himself away from all that sustained him, to go to her.

"David, come! She's waiting!"

I was possessed by a murderous rage. How dare he! He would lure Houle with this false mother's love back to the walls of some state institution for the insane. Houle was mine. I had saved him, I had fed and sheltered and loved him. Mr. Lindstrom had no right to do this dreadful thing.

I screamed. I shrieked with fury. I flew up over Mr. Lindstrom's head. They all looked up at me, outlined against the sky, Houle merely curious, Dawn and Mr.

Lindstrom openmouthed, shocked, at this bird of prey suddenly in their midst.

I dropped on Mr. Lindstrom, not silently as upon prey, but screeching like a demon, talons extended, ripping, tearing, slashing at Houle's enemy and therefore my enemy. I felt flesh tear and tasted blood. I wheeled away, flying low, heading for the tree.

I regained my perch, panting. I felt no remorse, not even when I saw Mr. Lindstrom clap a hand to his cheek and bring it away bloody. He was not my kind. How could I ever have thought it?

"*Dad?* Dad, are you okay? Dad?" Houle looked horrified.

Dad? No! I would not believe it. Mr. Lindstrom was not Houle's father. No, never!

But Houle had said so. Houle had called him "Dad." Well, and if he was, what of that? He was then as wicked and as uncaring as his coldhearted wife, Houle's mother. The pair of them, each worse than the other, plotting to bind my Houle and cast him into the pit.

"Houle!" I cried to him, with the last of my breath.

"Dad! Oh, Owl"—turning to me—"why did you do it?"

"Houle!" I cried, and then, I don't know why, I called aloud to him, a clear loud barn owl cry. It was the call of wife to husband, and husband to wife.

Come! Fly to me!

There is no call so insistent, so impossible to ignore. It is a cry from the heart to the heart, bypassing the mind, that jerks the shoulder muscles into flight without conscious effort. If the one you love calls you in this way, you cannot help it; you must come. I had never even heard the call before; till this moment I did not know I knew it. Yet I felt the power of it, I knew without being told.

Houle flinched as if struck. His arms made a faint swimming motion. He stepped away from his father, toward me.

Come! Fly to me!

Houle opened his mouth. A noise came out of it, strangled and strange.

His figure blurred. He shrank, he loomed large again and then dwindled. His arms grew great, sweeping sleeves, scalloped at the edges. The head rounded, the enormous eyes grew even larger in the heart-shaped face. His nose sharpened and hooked itself over his mouth. His legs, now clothed in feathery breeches, grew eight terrible claws at their tips and grasped at the wind.

He beat his great wings, once, twice, and rose into the air, leaving tattered, filthy clothing on the snow below him. He opened his mouth, now a proper beak, and replied: *I come! Wait for me!*

Joy streamed through me like moonlight through

clouds. Owls have no tear ducts, yet I swear I wept. He flew to me, awkward as a newly hatched owlet, and landed beside me on the branch. It was he, himself, the mad barn owl. My poor, darling Houle!

I saw it all now. He was a wereowl born to normal parents. (Was my mother right—were we distantly related?) How should he know how to hunt, to fly, the thousand things a wereowl must know? There was no one to teach him, as my parents had taught me. *They*—Mr. Lindstrom and the Wailing Woman—had thought him demented, when he tried to do what his instinct told him he must do. Yes of course! They had shut him up as a mad boy when he persisted, when he tried to catch the prey he must have, if he was to transform. How then could he prove them wrong, show evidence of his double nature, even to himself?

I contemplated my Houle's childhood with horror. Was that not enough to drive anyone mad in earnest? I know something by now of the human race. He would have been an object of fear and disgust even to those who loved him the most. His deepest, most vital needs would have made him a monster in their eyes and, eventually, in his own eyes as well.

Under these circumstances insanity would almost seem like a refuge, a safe harbor. And the only way to escape it would be to face his true identity—precisely the activity that had driven him mad in the first place.

Was he mad now? Was it too late for him? I turned and looked at him, swaying insecurely on the branch beside me. His eyes met mine, round and astonished, but as sane as my own.

Thankfulness buzzed in my head like a whole hive of bees. How brave was his mind and spirit; what a longing for life, for his own true nature, he had! He was not the weakling I had thought him. Alone, doubting himself as he must, he had escaped, had tried to teach himself to live in these wintry woods.

When I had taught him a thing or two, he would make such an owl as had not been seen in these woods for a century or more.

I heard a slight rustle below us. I was just about to drop on it when I realized that Houle had heard it too. His head pivoted around, searching for the exact location of the noise, then suddenly, noiselessly, he was gone. In less time than it takes to tell, he was back, a field mouse dangling from his beak. He bit the head off neatly and then shyly offered the body to me. His head bobbed nervously as he held it out, as though he feared I would not take it.

Of course I took it.

He had no idea what he was offering. He could not know that he was proposing to protect and feed me, as I would protect and feed him, to become the father of my children, the companion of my youth and old age, to stand by me all the days of our lives.

No, he didn't know, but I took him up on it anyway. You may think I have been blind or foolish about some of the events that have taken place within these pages, but I am not that big a fool.

"Hey, you! The big owl on the left. No, my left, not yours." It was Dawn, of course, breaking into this tender passage with typical tact.

"Yeah, you. I know who you are. The little one with the black eyes is Houle, or David, or whatever you want to call him. But you, you with the yellow eyes, you're my lab partner, aren't you?"

Ah yes. The humans. Something had to be done about these humans.

sixteen

I LOOKED BENEVOLENTLY DOWN UPON DAWN and Mr. Lindstrom. In spite of the fact that they were both vile, treacherous creatures, I felt quite kindly toward them at the moment.

Mr. Lindstrom sat in the snow gaping first at Houle and me and then at Dawn. He must be quite cold, I thought, without boots or jacket, the snow seeping through the seat of his trousers and the hole in his Hush Puppies. Dawn really ought to take better care of him than that if she hoped to keep him. Poor man, she was paying no attention to him at all. It was just as well he had the Wailing Woman as a backup. Dawn was standing, arms folded, staring hard at me.

"Well?" she demanded.

Conversations between members of different species are difficult at best. I decided that since the secret was out I might as well transform before these two. In human form I would be better able to warn them not to meddle with Houle. This branch was too slender to carry my weight as a human girl, so with a reassuring glance at Houle, I flew to a lower, larger one.

Entirely forgetting my previous problems with transformation, I slipped quickly and easily into my human shape.

Houle nearly fell off his branch. He gawked down at me, beak agape. A little strangled squawk emerged from him, and he fluttered his wings to keep his balance.

"It's all right, Houle," I called. "You see? We're birds of a feather, you and I."

I turned to look down at the humans from my perch on a sturdy tree limb about six feet off the ground.

"That's right," I said sternly. "We're birds of a feather, and we'll be flocking together from now on. We are not your kind, and you are not ours. I take responsibility for Houle."

Mr. Lindstrom got up slowly from the ground, brushing ice crystals off his behind. "Houle?" he said stupidly.

"She means David," Dawn said impatiently.

"What happened to David? Did you see that, Dawn? They—they're both *owls*, Dawn."

"I know. I saw."

"They *can't* be. It's not possible."

"Well they are," Dawn snapped.

Really, I had always thought Mr. Lindstrom was such an intelligent man. He certainly was having a hard time getting this, poor fellow.

"I suppose you did the best you could for him," I said

kindly, "but you really weren't equipped to be a parent to a wereowl." I was beginning to feel rather sorry for him. What *was* a human father to do with a child who insisted upon a steady diet of raw rodents, amphibians, and insects?

"My parents and I will care for him. You and the Wailing Woman need not worry. He'll be trained in all necessary life skills and enjoy a home life suited to his particular needs. You just carry on as you have been. No doubt you need some leisure time in which to sort out your personal life."

"The Wailing Woman?" he turned to Dawn for enlightenment. Dawn just shrugged.

"Your wife," I explained. "At least I assume it's your wife. That woman you were kissing last night." I watched Dawn carefully to see how she reacted to this.

Her eyebrows rose and she turned to look at Mr. Lindstrom, but she controlled her emotions admirably. You would think she had no interest beyond that of an ordinary student treated to an account of a teacher's sex life.

"Yes . . . yes," Mr. Lindstrom answered, with an uncomfortable look at Dawn. "That was my wife, as a matter of fact. She was . . . we were both very worried about David. We're sorry if our being so, ah, demonstrative, caused you any concern."

"Certainly not."

And, do you know? That wasn't a lie. Oh I admit I was a little upset at the time, but it was nothing to me now. In fact, my infatuation with Houle's father was beginning to seem a bit grotesque. He was so old, for one thing.

What about an owl's faithfulness unto death? you might ask. Well, we never really were engaged, you know. No bonding had taken place. That widower owl tried to court me, but when I did not respond to his overtures, I suppose he went off and courted somebody else.

Then too, I am half human. Humans seem to need a little practice at romantic love before they really settle down. And since Houle wasn't there, I chose his father as the next best thing. So I hope you will not think me too fickle.

"So it was the Bird Man here you were after all the time," Dawn burst out, "and not—"

"You needn't worry," I said hastily. Even though it was all over, I didn't want Houle or his father to know about my silly schoolgirl crush. "He's all yours," I added generously.

"All mine?" Dawn asked, with a creased brow.

"Well, yours and his wife's, anyway. I admit his being married is a bit of a disadvantage, but that relationship seems fairly shaky. I'd say you at least have a fighting chance."

"What are you talking about?" Dawn asked.

I sighed. She was usually so quick.

Dawn went on.

"Do you mean Steve? He isn't married. He's only fifteen. Anyway, what do you know about Steve?" Dawn's face darkened with suspicion.

"Steve? No, no. I have it on excellent authority that his name is John. And you're the one who told me he was forty. Don't be silly, Dawn. He couldn't be fifteen."

"Not Mr. Lindstrom, Steve Moran. That's who I—" Dawn reddened and became abruptly silent.

"Steve Moran? That nitwit whose locker is right next to mine? You're in love with him?"

Dawn's pink face became even pinker. She looked almost pretty. "No! Not exactly. Well . . . he's not that bad, Owl. He's smarter than you think. He's just shy, so he acts kinda gooney."

"Then why did you give Mr. Lindstrom here a love potion?" I demanded, pointing at the gentleman in question with the toe of my sneaker.

Mr. Lindstrom looked a little startled at this.

"For you, you dope! I thought you were—"

"Oh! I see!" I interrupted quickly.

"And, Owl, I'm sorry to tell you this, but that stuff is absolutely worthless. If they weren't your parents, I'd be screaming for my money back. I bought some for Mr. Lindstrom, and some for . . . well, some for Steve, too. I had to pound up this tablet and put it together with one of your body parts—"

"What!"

"Keep your shirt on. I just used one of your hairs. I found it in my brush from when you were over that day. I cut it up really fine and mixed it with the powder into a chocolate from a box of candy. I got one of those little heart-shaped boxes left over from Valentine's Day. It seemed appropriate. Then I stuck it into his mailbox. I did the same thing with Steve, only with my hair."

"Those chocolates . . ." Mr. Lindstrom touched his stomach tenderly with his hand. He looked a little sick.

"You did eat them, then? All of them?" Dawn asked.

"Er, yes. I have rather a sweet tooth. I thought—well, frankly, I hoped it was from my wife. She left me about six months ago. Because of David, of course; all our differences have stemmed from David's . . . illness. So of course I ate it. I was sorry afterward. The heartburn! And hiccups! I've had them for days. I have them still, I—" He halted and stood for a moment, listening intently to his inner workings.

Dawn laughed. "No, you don't. Owl scared them out of you."

I was very embarrassed. I did not know how to explain what my father had done, and why. "The, er, love potion is not perhaps the best spell my parents have to offer."

"I'll say!" sniffed Dawn. "Steve never looked at me even once. He just hiccuped."

"Well, after all, you wouldn't really want him just to like you because of some powder in a piece of candy, would you?" I asked.

"Sure," Dawn said. "How else do you think I'll ever get a guy?"

I would have responded to this, but a sudden thought struck me. "If you're not in love with Mr. Lindstrom, why did you betray Houle to him? Why did you betray our friendship?"

Dawn's face reddened again. "Listen, Owl. I didn't betray anybody. I followed you when you left my house last night. I saw Mr. Lindstrom stop and talk to you, all upset. I heard what he said. It was pretty obvious who Houle was then. You didn't have the right to keep him from proper medical care, and you didn't have the right to keep him away from his parents, either. I'll bet he's still underage."

Mr. Lindstrom nodded. "He's fifteen."

"I was going to tell you this morning in school, but you didn't show up. So I decided enough was enough. I walked all the way back here—me, I walked four miles— to tell Mr. Lindstrom where we'd hidden his son."

I was silent a moment. "You could have let me know," I said. "I couldn't have prevented you from telling anyone."

Dawn looked away. "I said you weren't there to tell."

"You could have stopped at my house. It was on your way."

"Yeah," Dawn said softly. "I guess I could have."

"Why didn't you?"

"Because! Because I guess I was mad at you."

"Why?" For some reason I experienced a nasty sensation at the pit of my stomach.

"Oh, Owl! We're supposed to be friends, right? Well, I was doing all the work in our friendship, you know that? Here I was, knocking myself out to try to help you, with Mr.—" She glanced quickly at Mr. Lindstrom and then away. "With your love life, and you wouldn't even let on if it was Mr.—who it was you were after. And then this business with Houle. You were using me, Owl. I ran a lot of risks for you, and you never told me one single thing that was going on. Why couldn't you tell me? I was a better friend to you than you deserved, Owl. You know why you didn't know about Steve Moran? Because you never asked. You weren't interested."

Dawn broke off here to fumble around in her purse for a tissue. To my horror I saw two fat tears rolling down her cheeks. I jumped down from the tree limb and approached her cautiously.

"I'm sorry, Dawn. Friendship does not come easily to—to people like me. I trusted you more than I have ever trusted anyone outside of my own family. I did appreciate all you did for Houle and me, truly I did. I am very sorry now that you are unhappy and that you are angry with me. I didn't know."

Dawn waved this away, averting her face from my gaze so that I might not see more tears following the first.

"Oh, you're right, I guess. It was a mean thing to do. I was mad, and kind of jealous in a way. You can hate me if you want to. I deserve it."

Shyly I reached out a hand and touched Dawn on the sleeve. "I don't hate you, Dawn."

Dawn scrubbed vigorously at her face with a crumpled tissue. "No," she said, practically, "I suppose you don't. Things have worked out pretty well for you."

Mr. Lindstrom cleared his throat. "Excuse me," he said hesitantly, "but I would like to speak to David, if I may."

Dawn and I looked up rather startled. I think we had both forgotten about the presence of the males for the past few minutes.

"David!" Mr. Lindstrom called up to Houle. "David, may I talk to you, please?"

Houle swooped silently to the wide branch I had recently abandoned. He began to transform, slowly, painfully.

He clearly still found it difficult. Within no more than a minute, however, he had become once again the dark, brooding boy of the woods. He was shivering, because of course he was as naked as a mushroom. Dawn made a noise midway between a giggle and a gasp. I swiftly tossed his clothes to him. He jumped to the ground, slipped around the tree trunk, and donned his shirt and pants while we all discreetly looked the other way.

"David!" Mr. Lindstrom cried as he emerged.

The boy drew himself up.

"My name is Houle," he said coldly.

"I see," Mr. Lindstrom said after a moment. "Does that mean that you don't want to come back with me?"

"Of course I don't. My life is here in the woods with Owl. Is that really your name?" he asked me, turning away from his father.

I nodded.

"Why didn't you ever let me know what you were? It would have made things so much easier."

I opened my mouth. How to explain my early distrust of him and my later inability, all in a moment? Instead I retorted, "I might ask you the same thing!"

"I didn't know that the owl and the girl were the same! You weren't exactly friendly when we were both owls. We're not a very chummy bunch, are we?" he added ruefully. "And I had no idea why you and that other girl were hiding me. I sure didn't trust you enough to transform in front of you. It's much harder for me than for you, I think. While I was sick it was practically impossible."

I nodded again. "Poor diet in your formative years," I said, and looked reproachfully at Mr. Lindstrom.

Mr. Lindstrom was smiling faintly. "That's the longest speech I believe I've ever heard out of Dav— out of Houle. I'm amazed I never noticed the similarities between you and Owl before."

Houle bowed his head in stiff courtesy toward his father. "That's because we are of the same kind." His eyes blazed silver for a moment. He held himself proudly, with a new self-confidence I had not seen in him before.

"I don't blame you, or my mother, for not knowing about me. It would be too much to expect."

"I can't so easily forgive myself," Mr. Lindstrom murmured. "There are traditions in our family about a curse, of all the crazy things. A strange condition that crops up every few generations. I thought it was some peculiar hereditary disease. I have wondered, more than once, if you were a victim of it."

Houle smiled at me. "Once, but no longer. Owl will teach me to enjoy it, rather than flee from it."

"You were learning that before I ever saw you," I said.

Houle shook his head. "To accept it, yes, to claim my identity. There was very little enjoyment in starving alone in the snow."

He turned toward his father. "Goodbye," he said. "Perhaps we will meet again. Say hello to my mother for me, and tell her I am happy."

"But wait, David—I mean Houle—won't you tell her yourself?"

Houle shook his head. "What would be the point? We have nothing to offer each other, except regrets for the past. I know you meant well. You must learn to forget me, and I hope, forgive me for causing you so much sorrow. Goodbye."

"Hold it." It was Dawn. She had melted gracefully into the background while Houle and his father and I talked, but now she elbowed her way back to center stage. "Don't let him do it, Owl. It's a big mistake."

"I don't understand," I said. "I think that what he says is true. It may seem hard to you, but it is true."

"Oh, pooh. So you two will just flap your wings and fly off into the woods forever and ever, eh? What about school?"

"School?" I said, somewhat taken aback.

"You're only fourteen. He's only fifteen. Forgetting any other considerations, it's the law."

"Very well, we will attend school from my parents' home."

"I notice you just assume that will be hunky-dory with your parents. Okay, okay," Dawn said, raising a hand as I opened my mouth with assurances. "Maybe a live-in boyfriend is just what Mom and Pop have always wanted for their teenage daughter. Lord knows they're weird enough. But neither of you is ready to get married yet, right? If I understand the situation, Houle is a long way from being ready to support a family."

"Yes," I agreed. "That is true. We will need to wait some years until he becomes sufficiently skilled."

"You're going to live under the same roof for a few years without . . . you know, starting a family?"

I blushed. Houle stared at his feet.

"Well . . ."

"You say he and his folks have nothing in common these days," she said, shifting ground. "No old business to take care of, right? No resentments, no guilt?"

We nodded uncertainly.

"Then why did he come here when he busted out of the loony bin?"

"Well . . ."

"What do you think will happen if he just cuts that part of his personality off? He's half human too, you know. You've got your family. Let him have his."

Houle shifted uneasily and looked at his father.

"I mean it, Owl. Don't let him do it. Make him go home and sort things out with his mom and dad." She turned to Houle. "You say you don't blame them for not knowing, so prove it. Now they know; give them a chance. Your dad's a biologist. I bet he could find out a lot about owls in no time."

Mr. Lindstrom cleared his throat again. "I could," he agreed. "And so could your mother. We want you at home, son. We always have."

Houle looked at me. I looked at Houle.

"Dawn's usually right," I said.

Houle no longer looked self-assured. He looked frightened.

"Yes, all right." But he caught up my hand in a fierce grip.

Mr. Lindstrom reached out a hand and touched his son lightly on the shoulder. "Thank you, son. And thank you, Dawn. Thank you very much," he murmured.

He looked at each of us in turn and then began to laugh, a little shakily.

"I have absolutely no idea how I'm ever going to explain this to my wife. You'd all better come home with us. I don't think we could separate Owl and Da— Houle without surgery at the moment anyway. I'm cold, and Houle must be too. You've been sick, haven't you?"

"He has," I agreed. "Let's get him home."

As we crunched back across the icy lawn, I murmured, "Dawn?"

"Yeah?"

"Maybe next we should start thinking about Steve Moran."

Dawn ducked her head. "Oh forget that. Sorry I mentioned it."

"No. I have an idea . . ."